Other Books

By Beryl Wealand

Snakebite
Diamondback
A Course in Terrorism

BERYL WEALAND

A CHILDISH DEATH

—⚶—

A Novel

An Arkansas River Valley Mystery

Pairodocs
Russellville & Dover, Arkansas

D
DOC
C

A Childish Death
By Beryl Wealand
Copyright 2017 © by P.B.W. Pendergrass

Notice of Rights

Author's Note

This is a work of fiction. Many of the characters are alter egos created individually by relatives and friends. Some are composites, but none are real individuals. All events and locations are either fictitious or are used fictitiously.

ISBN-13: 9780999063002
ISBN-10: 0999063006
Library of Congress Control Number: 2017909821
Pairodocs, Dover, AR

Cover Design by Paula B. Pendergrass
Cover Photograph by Paula B. Pendergrass
Graphic Art by Katelynn McAlister

DEDICATION

This book is dedicated to those among us who soldier on, enduring and overcoming the taint of child molestation and child pornography.

WHEN BENNIE SUE WAS EIGHT

1

The trial had been going on for almost a week and the Prosecutor was all but finished. One thing remained for this late October court: the testimony of the child. The jury and the court spectators were silent as the side door opened and a small girl, accompanied by her *Guardian ad Litum*, entered the courtroom and approached the witness box. She wore a brand new dress in this year's colors of blue and pink, and a pink scrunchie held her shiny light brown hair in a ponytail. She kept her head down, looking at her purple and pink tennies. Unaware of her impact on the observers, this small angel stepped up into the box and seated herself, calmly smoothing down her skirt and straightening her shoulders. She was as ready as she would ever be.

As the *Guardian* took her seat at the table, the prosecuting attorney moved toward the girl slowly and quietly, as if she were a small bird he didn't wish to scare away. She gave her name, Bennie Sue Blackwell, raised her right hand and solemnly swore to tell the truth when the Bailiff asked. As she spoke, the audience could see the gap where a bottom bicuspid was missing. Then she clenched her hands and looked down at her lap, afraid to look directly at either her mother, or at the defendant, James Blackwell.

The prosecutor started slowly, trying to build her confidence and gain her trust. Perhaps he had made a mistake in choosing to have her testify. Child witnesses could be very unreliable, and the whole situation could be traumatic. But he had sensed a solidness about this little girl, enough so that he was willing to risk it. He asked her where she went to school, if she had a pet, and when her birthday was. She told him she was eight, but was going to be nine this summer, and she wanted a puppy for her present.

Then he asked her if she knew why she was here.

"Yes," she nodded her head. "I'm here because my daddy has been bad."

"Has he been bad to other people, or just you?" he asked for clarification.

"I think it's mostly just me," she replied somberly.

"What did your daddy do to you that was bad?" he held his breath hoping for a clear response. About 90% of child witnesses clammed up on the witness stand.

"He put his fingers inside my bottom," she whispered just loudly enough for the court to hear.

"Was this just one time?" he continued.

"No, he kept doing it at night when my mommy was working. I told him I didn't like it, but he said it would help me grow up faster. I guess it works because everybody says I'm growing like a weed."

"Did it hurt you?"

"Not after the first couple of times when I cried. He told me I was a brave girl, and that if I didn't tell anybody, he'd let me look at his pictures."

"Can you tell us about the pictures?"

"He had them in a secret place in his closet. Him and me were the only ones who got to see them."

"What did they look like?"

"They were mostly pictures of girls with their panties off."

"Were there any boys?"

"Yeah, there were three. They weren't wearing any underwear either."

"Were there any grownups?"

"No, it was just kids."

"Thank you Bennie. I have no further questions." He returned to the table and sat with his head down.

The defense attorney declined to question the witness, and the *Guardian ad Litum* escorted her from the courtroom.

—⚏—

It took the jury only 30 minutes to convict James Blackwell. But the sentencing phase took a lot longer. The jury would hear testimony from affected parties then deliberate on a sentence of from 20 to 100 years.

The pre-sentencing testimony was basically predictable and did little to change the jurors' comprehension of the situation. Friends from work testified that the defendant was a good worker and friend. One woman testified that she had never known him to do or say anything disrespectful to women he worked with. The minister testified that the Blackwell's were a good, young Christian family who deserved as much forgiveness and mercy as the jury could see fit to provide. Bennie Sue's mother, Della, testified that James was a good husband and daddy, and that the girls needed their father. The case worker from the Department of Human Services testified that the emotional damage to Bennie Sue, while certain, could not be adequately calculated. A lot depended on Bennie Sue's own perception of herself as a victim.

The cyber-specialist from the police department testified that the jury should keep in mind that child pornography was a heinous crime against minors. It wasn't just about looking at some dirty pictures. He pointed out that child pornography, unlike adult pornography, was almost always a depiction of child abuse, pure and simple. Small children were being violated and sexually abused for the benefit of the voyeurs who traded in child porn. Children were being betrayed by the adults who should be protecting them. This testimony was supported by a psychologist from Little Rock who had experience with Child Protective Services and CASA. He had been a strong advocate for abused children in his own part of the state, but he was not well known in the River Valley. Hence, his testimony was additive, but not especially important to the jury.

The jurors discussed their ideas in a calm manner. This was not a jury of hotheads. Nor was it a jury of prudes. One man went straight for the 100 year mark. His reasoning was simple: Anyone who did that to a child then forced her to look at pictures of other children being abused should be removed from this earth. A sentence of 100 years was fair enough! One of the women jurors countered that her sister had been raped as a child and had come through it very well. She leaned toward 20 years.

A compromise was reached. Considering that Arkansas felons were eligible for parole after serving 70% of their sentence, and considering that the main goal was to keep Mr. Blackwell from harming any of his children (there was an 18 month old toddler at home now), a 30 year sentence seemed appropriate. Both his daughters would be grown by the time he was likely to be released in 21 years.

2

Life became Hell for Bennie Sue after the trial during the next two months before the Christmas break. There was a regular gauntlet at school. The older boys on the bus started it, and soon the others joined in. It started as soon as she climbed the steps. "Bennie Sue's old man is a jail bird. Wonder if they'll 'do' him the way he did her." "Bennie Sue likes to look at dirty pictures!" "Here comes Bennie Sue wearing a dress. Now we can fuck her." "Nah, who'd want to fuck her; her old man already did." The bus driver did what she could by assigning Bennie Sue to the seat immediately behind her. Bennie Sue still took hits from other students as they passed her getting on and off, but her tormentors were not nearly so foul mouthed with an adult in hearing range.

The halls at school were no better. Fortunately Bennie Sue's third grade class stayed in their own room most of the day. And her teacher, Mrs. Ponder, was quick to shut down any sniping. But Bennie Sue dreaded going to the lunch room where somebody might catcall, "Hey Bennie Sue, you still datin' older men?" Then a whole table of students would snicker at her.

The thing that was hard to understand was that people kept treating her as if she had done something wrong, something nasty. Sometimes she was in tears when her CASA volunteer stopped by to check on her. When was this going to end?

—◊—

Bennie Sue wasn't the only one suffering. Her mother, Della, was up against it too. When James Blackwell went to prison, her whole world went bump in the night. James had been the main bread winner, and being an engineer, he commanded a good salary. She and the girls had lived off savings and James' last check while he was in jail. Ever the engineer, James had figured that if they bailed him out at $200,000 cash, there wouldn't be anything for his family to live on. So he had elected to stay in the Pope County Detention Center. Now the verdict was final, and most of the money was gone. Della's choices were easy, but the pain was hard.

Della could make enough as an RN to support herself and her girls, but at a much lower standard of living then she currently enjoyed. First, the house had to go. She put it on the market at a reduced price hoping for a quick sale. When all the new assessments and new surveys required by the lender, and the minor repairs required by the buyers, and the miscellaneous costs were figured in, she walked away from a very nice house, with a little less than $3,000.

Della couldn't sell the brand new Beemer for enough to pay it off, and she couldn't find anyone to take over payments, so she let the finance company repossess it. The day they came for the car, she walked outside with her head up, trying to convince the neighbors that she was handling the situation gracefully. Then she went back into the house and bawled for an hour.

It took Della several weeks to find an affordable two-bedroom mobile home in an older park between Lamar and Clarksville. That meant Bennie Sue would have to change schools from Pope to Johnson County. Della thought it would be for the best. Bennie Sue's teachers had let her know about the continuing harassment at her current school. They'd wait to make the move after Christmas. Meanwhile, Della dropped Bennie Sue off at school early in the mornings, and Aunt Alexis picked her up in the afternoon. Bennie Sue was relieved not to have to ride the bus, but she still walked down the hall with her head down, hoping not to draw attention. And the lunchroom was still an ordeal.

Della had always said the there were two things that could ruin your life, unreliable transportation and unreliable child care. Her old Toyota Camry needed new tires, but so far it was running reliably. She lucked into a daycare opening for Cheyenne, her toddler. And they would allow Bennie Sue to stay there in the afternoons.

Della wasn't working nights anymore. She had to be there with the girls. Johnson County Medical offered her a flexible day shift, and she took it. The pay was a little less, but everyone at St. Mary's in Pope County knew what had happened, and quite a few of them blamed her. A fresh start would do her good.

Della's coworkers at St. Mary's weren't the only ones who blamed her. She blamed herself. She had been abused by her own father and felt she could recognize the symptoms in other girls. Why had she missed Bennie Sue? Hadn't her daughter complained about itching "down there"? And Della, a nurse, of all people, hadn't even looked at what turned out to be a scabby ring around the little girl's vagina. She'd never forget the humiliation when the doctor and the social worker had called her in for a conference to inform her. She had been so busy with her work and her toddler, feeling certain that Bennie Sue was doing fine without very much of her attention, that she hadn't even bothered to check!

3

The January move to Johnson County schools was a godsend for Bennie Sue. Now her momma could drop her off and pick her up after school. The ladies at the daycare had been nice to her, but she really wanted to have some personal time with Della before they picked Cheyenne up. Sometimes they'd drive all the way down Rogers Avenue to the McDonalds for French fries and a diet cola. Della tried to control sugar intake for the whole family. A small cone or sundae would have been nice too, but habits were habits.

After they got home, Bennie Sue played with Cheyenne, often taking her out to the old beat-up swing set the previous owners had abandoned on the lot. Then the two of them would watch cartoons or play a video. Cheyenne never got tired of *Cinderella*. Sometimes they'd draw (or scribble) or color in the books Mom's sister, Aunt Alexis, brought for them. Bennie Sue loved to read, and she'd read aloud until Cheyenne dozed off with a pacifier in her mouth.

While Bennie Sue was babysitting Cheyenne, Della had a little time to herself, although she couldn't leave them alone and go to the store, or for a ride, or to a bar, or any of the things she had been used to doing. Sometimes she resented the girls, and it made her feel guilty. Then she'd get mad at James all over again and wish she'd never met him. Sometimes late at night when she was lying in her bed, alone and longing for arms around her, she'd forgive him and wish that he could come home.

Bennie Sue set the table every night while Della prepared dinner. They ate a lot of frozen prepared things. Pizza was everybody's favorite. Bennie Sue helped with the cleanup and dishes, and the three of them would watch early evening TV. Bennie Sue got to watch some programs by herself while Della bathed Cheyenne and put her to bed. The two girls were sharing a double bed now in a crowded little room with a bathroom in the hall. Mom's room had a bigger bathroom with a small Jacuzzi that was really neat when it filled up with bubbles.

Bennie Sue was hungry for new friends. Della was hungry for a man. Bennie Sue fed her hunger with reading. Della filled hers with liquor. But not in front of the girls. She could usually hold off until the girls were in bed, but when the drive hit her early, she had learned to drink tea, Long Island iced tea, that is.

—〰—

The kids at school didn't torment Bennie Sue. She could walk from one end of the hall to the other without any sexually suggestive remarks being made. Sure, quite a few of the kids knew something had gone wrong at her previous school. Some thought she had blown the whistle on a cheating ring; some thought she'd punched a teacher; most thought that her dad had run out on her family, and her mother had been forced to move because she couldn't pay her rent (closer to the truth than they knew). This latter rumor was the one that stuck. No big deal. There were as many students here with only one parent as with two.

4

In February warm days came more often, and the students at Bennie Sue's school began to spend more of their recess time outdoors. Bennie Sue liked the swings where she could soar out over the grass and pretend she could fly. She would have spent all her time on the swings, but there was usually a line, so she had to yield like everyone else.

One day when she was standing near the jungle gym (Della had strongly warned her about getting on and falling off), she was approached by a girl in her home room, Beth Ann. "You're the new girl," she stated matter-of-factly. "I heard your daddy was in jail."

Bennie Sue froze. She had become very sensitive about her situation and didn't want to talk about it to this girl.

"That's all right," Beth Ann continued. "It's not your fault. My name's Beth Ann. I sit way behind you in Mrs. Tucker's home room, and we have lunch and recess together. Want to play hopscotch?"

Bennie Sue nodded, and the two girls skipped across to the sidewalk where now- faded hopscotch squares had been painted several years ago. They hopped in the squares until they tired of that then moved toward the hula hoops, but recess was over before they got their turns.

Bennie Sue was well aware of who Beth Ann was. She was one of the "popular" girls in her school. She had really nice clothes, and her mother let her bleach two streaks, one on either side of her face, in her light brown hair. Although she was just in third grade like Bennie Sue, she was close friends with two fourth graders, Tosha and Nikki. They called themselves the Three Musketeers and went everywhere together.

The next day at lunch, Bennie Sue was walking slowly with her tray, looking for a solitary place to sit. Sometimes she sat with the "nobodies" who collected at a couple of long tables in the back of the cafetorium. She sighed and headed that way when she saw Beth Ann waving at her. The Three Musketeers and a couple of other fourth graders were at a table by the windows. Bennie Sue kept her head down and angled toward the popular girls. She didn't lift her head until she reached their table and was fully prepared to keep on walking toward a table with only three students farther down the wall.

"Hey, Skinny Bennie," Beth Ann's voice reached her, "where ya goin'?" When Bennie Sue dared to look up, Beth Ann waved her over to sit beside her. "This is Skinny Bennie," Beth Ann informed the others who were staring at Bennie Sue with puzzled looks on their faces. "She's in my home room class, and her daddy's in jail." Bennie Sue blushed bright red. She wanted to say something clever to make the truth go away, but her tongue froze just as it had yesterday on the playground.

"Don't worry," Beth Ann reassured the others. "I checked her out on the playground yesterday. She's OK." Beth Ann completely ignored the other students toward the end of the table and introduced Tosha and Nikki. "We're the Three Musketeers. We go everywhere together and do everything together." The three girls smiled at some inside joke. "We're going to ride our bikes out to the Brickyard after school. Wanna come?" Bennie Sue wanted nothing more, but she was too embarrassed to tell them she didn't even own a bicycle. "That sounds really great," she faked it, "but my mom picks me up after school and we go to McDonalds." At least that part was true.

"Wow, what a neat mom!" Tosha approved. "I wish my mom got off work in time to take me, or all of us (she indicated the Three Musketeers) to McDonalds."

"My mom's a nurse," Bennie Sue felt she needed to explain why her mother was available to pick her up. Quite a few of the mothers here didn't work, but relied on welfare to get them through while the Department of Human Services (DHS) tried to hunt down the delinquent fathers. "She has to go in really early, but she gets afternoons off to spend with us." Bennie Sue didn't tell them she spent most afternoons baby sitting her little sister while Mom took some personal time.

That night Bennie Sue worked up enough courage to ask Della about getting a bike. Della's first response, as usual, was "No. We can't afford one." But then she took an interest in the request and asked Bennie Sue why she suddenly needed a bike.

"Well," Bennie Sue stammered, "there are some girls at school that ride bikes together. And they asked me if I'd like to come along. Please, Mom, I'll take good care of it and chain it up so it won't get stolen."

"Let me think about it," Della gave in just a little. The longing in Bennie Sue's eyes nearly broke her heart. Later that night after the girls were in bed, Della called an old friend who was a member of Kiwanis and told her about Bennie Sue's request. The friend was noncommittal, but promised to look into it. Kiwanis usually gave away several bikes at their spring Easter egg hunt. Maybe something could be worked out.

—⁂—

The new bike was wonderful! It was a stripped down version, but it was new, and it was turquoise with a small book basket on the front. There was no fender over the back wheel so Bennie Sue would not be taking anyone along on a ride. In fact, Bennie Sue herself would not be going for a ride. She didn't know how to ride a bike. She used to have a little pink scooter before the move to the trailer, but it was too hard to ride on the grass and gravel around here.

Bennie Sue spent all her time after school learning to ride. She'd sit Cheyenne in the glider on the swing then ride back and forth on the little dirt road beside the trailer. She took a lot of falls since she was self taught. Della was usually inside drinking her spiked tea. Bennie Sue was determined; before long she was making sharp turns at the ends of the little road. Once when Cheyenne was inside, she rode down to the end of the trailer court where a new block of tar and gravel had just been laid. The tar was still soft, and Bennie Sue took a bad fall, landing on one knee. She ignored the scrape and walked her bike back home, too jelly-legged to climb back on.

As Bennie Sue pushed her bike, she realized it had tar on it from when it had fallen. Della would be furious! Bennie Sue snuck into the kitchen for paper towels and managed to clean most of the tar off. Della came out to look for her as she was wiping the spokes. "Bennie Sue what are you doing?" her tone was harsh.

Bennie Sue ducked her head and spoke flatly, "I got some tar on my bike."

"How did you manage to do that?"

"I fell down there where they put on tar and gravel." Bennie Sue pointed. She expected the next question to be about why she was down there in the first place, but Della surprised her.

"Are you all right? That must have been a nasty fall." Della came down the little steps and helped Bennie Sue finish wiping the tar off the bike. " Let's see that knee. I took a fall just about like that once. We never could get all the tar out from under my skin, and I still have that scar to this day."

Bennie Sue was proud of her bandage the next day at school. It didn't mean she was stupid. It meant that for the first time in a long time Della was taking care of her.

5

When Della was confident that Bennie Sue could be trusted not to wreck her bike, she plotted a safe "back way" for Bennie Sue to ride to school. The first morning, she followed closely in the car, making sure Bennie Sue followed all the rules of the road (and that no one bothered her). Bennie Sue's instructions were to come straight home from school. Della would pick up Cheyenne, and they would meet at the trailer.

Bennie Sue was very proud and excited to show the Three Musketeers her new bike. Now she could go riding with them (if Della would let her). The three were very under-whelmed. Their bikes were much more expensive and had five gears in comparison to the three on Bennie Sue's bike. Tosha recognized the disappointment on Bennie Sue's face and made it somewhat better by patting the turquoise bike and commenting "It'll do. I love the color."

The new bike was not the entry into the world of the Three Musketeers that Bennie Sue longed for. She still sat with them at lunch, but it was clear that she was not part of their world. They had so many secrets and inside jokes that left Bennie Sue on the outside looking in. Besides she had to go straight home every day to baby-sit.

Then the barrier lowered slightly. "We're going to have a little party at my house Friday after school," Beth Ann offered. "Ask your mom if you can come. We'll have you home by 5:00. Promise."

To Bennie Sue's surprise, Della agreed. Friday was a warm sunny day, and the turquoise bike seemed to float all the way to school.

Bennie Sue followed the others a little less than a mile to a development of nice brick houses. Beth Ann's house was made of a soft brown brick with white and gold shutters and doors. It wasn't so nice as the house Bennie Sue had lived in before the trial, but she admired it terribly and wished she could live in a nice house again.

Bennie Sue was surprised when Beth Ann matter-of-factly took out a key and opened the front door. "Where's your mom?" she asked curiously.

"Oh, she'll be here after while. She works late on Fridays. It's OK. I have friends over all the time."

"I love your house", Bennie Sue gushed. "Which one is your bedroom?"

Beth Ann moved to the door of a room down the hall. It was perfect! The walls were mint green on three sides with the wall behind the canopy bed papered in pastel butterfly print (no pink princess here; that was so passé). The dresser and matching chest were white rattan, and the matching rocking chair was filled with stuffed animals.

"This is so neat!" Bennie Sue exclaimed. "You are so lucky."

"Oh, it'll do," Beth Ann dismissed the compliment. "The really neat stuff is in my mom's room." She ushered the little group of girls farther down the hall. Although she was only nine, and the other two Musketeers were ten, it was clear she was the queen bee.

As soon as Beth Ann opened the door the Three Musketeers ran and jumped on the king-size bed. "Pillow fight!" Nikki yelled, and the three of them pulled pillows and cushions from the made up bed and began pummeling each other in earnest. The bed was an absolute mess when they had finished and lay giggling across the center. "Won't your mom get you?" Bennie Sue asked in amazement.

"Nah, she doesn't care, just as long as we don't bust anything," Beth Ann responded. "Now, who wants to get sexy?" She moved across to one of the dressers and began opening drawers. "Here, Tosha, try this," she flung a silky night gown at her friend. "Nikki, try the red. The pink's for me, and Bennie Sue, you get the black," she held out a lacy black slip toward Bennie who was glued to the floor. As the others began stripping out of their school clothes and wiggling into the nightwear, Beth Ann took some photos with her new digital camera. She scolded Bennie Sue, "come on, girl. It's a dress up party, and you need to dress up."

While Bennie Sue slipped out of her clothes, turning to the wall so the others wouldn't see her naked chest, Beth Ann moved on toward the small dressing table in the hall leading into the enormous bathroom. She began opening drawers again, pulling out an assortment of cosmetics. "Mom's got some new shades," she announced as she painted her lips with a narrow tube of lipstick. "This one is 'shimmering firelight'; how does it look?" The other two Musketeers picked 'sumptuous watermelon' and 'night moves' expertly applying the lipstick while Bennie Sue stood watching dumbly. "Here, Bennie Sue, this one's perfect for you." Beth Ann put one hand on Bennie Sue's shoulder and applied 'pink dreams' to her friend's lips.

The four little girls took turns strutting across the bedroom floor and posing in front of the full-length mirrors. Tosh, at 10, was the oldest, and she was beginning to get breast buds, so when she stuck her chest out ostentatiously, the others were secretly jealous. Bennie Sue, who was still eight, was the least developed of the group. The black slip kept sliding off her shoulders revealing her flat nipples so she held it up with one hand while she tried to vamp with the other. Meanwhile Beth Ann was taking pictures with the digital camera. Bennie Sue had never been to a party like this.

They were back in their school clothes and moving toward the kitchen for something to drink when Bennie Sue noticed the clock. She had to scurry. It was already 4:30. Della had said 5:00, and

Della meant 5:00. She hurried out of the house and biked back past the school and onto her familiar streets, arriving just in time to see her mom getting out of the car.

"Hi," Della said as she leaned into the back seat to release Cheyenne. "You're cutting it pretty close aren't you?" Then she looked at Bennie Sue. "Young lady, what is that on your face? And your blouse?"

Bennie Sue looked at a streak of 'pink dreams' on her sleeve. "It's lipstick." Bennie Sue knew she'd never be allowed to use her mother's things the way the girls had used things at Beth Ann's house. "Her mother lets her play with it. I had a really good time. We played dress-up." No further details were forthcoming.

"Well, OK. I guess," Della was noncommittal. "But next time take it off before you come home. You know you're not supposed to wear it outside the house."

6

There was no mention of a party during the next week of school although it was clear to Bennie Sue that the Three Musketeers were planning something together. It was disappointing, but not tragic, especially since it was pouring down rain on Friday. The three were whisked away by one of the moms, and Bennie Sue waited patiently for Della to come for her and her bicycle according to their agreed upon rain plan.

The next Thursday, Beth Ann invited Bennie Sue to come to her house after school Friday for a pizza party. Della agreed, and Bennie Sue put on her best under panties in case they played dress up again. Beth Ann pretended to be calling home, but ordered the pizza from the office phone just before they left school on their bikes. That way they wouldn't lose any party time waiting for an order.

Beth Ann unlocked her front door and let them in. Bennie Sue asked about her mom, and Beth Ann shrugged her off with "Oh, she'll be home later. She told me to go ahead." She held up a $20.00 bill that had been left in the front hall for the pizza. "She lets me order pizza all the time. Let's get ready."

The pizza delivery boy was truly surprised, and his eye brows lifted high when the front door was opened by four little girls in lipstick, earrings, and boas. "Oh, hi," Beth Ann was the spokesperson for the group. "Did you have any trouble finding us?" They were all staring at him and giggling.

"Uh, no" he regained his composure. "Pepperoni, no anchovies?" When Beth Ann nodded, he continued, "that'll be $12.95."

"Would you like to step in while I get the money?" Beth Ann asked in what she thought was her most sultry voice.

"Uh, no ma'am, we're not allowed to come inside. If one of you could just take the pizza."

Tosha held the pizza while Beth Ann picked up the bill from the hall table.

"Here you go, sweetie," she simpered at him, pulling the bill out of the front of her shirt. "You can keep the change."

He took the proffered bill and nodded his head in her direction. "Thank you very much ma'am. We hope you'll call us again."

"Oh, we will," she said breathlessly. "You can bet on that!"

He blushed and hurried to his little delivery truck.

As soon as the door closed, four girls burst into whoops and giggles. "He called you ma'am. Did you see him blush? Do you think he liked us?"

They ate their pizza on paper plates at the kitchen table along with cola served in very fancy stemware from the hutch in the dining room. Bennie Sue was pretty sure Della had some pretty stems in a cardboard box in the little storage shed out back. Maybe they could unwrap just three of them and use them for special occasions.

The chatter was centered on the delivery boy. He was a local teenager, old enough to have a driver's license. The girls didn't know it, but he was working after school to save money for his own car.

"Oh, man, wasn't he handsome?" Nikki started. "He can deliver pizza to me any time!"

"You were sooo sexy, Beth Ann," Tosha added.

"I guess so," Beth Ann pretended she didn't care. "But he doesn't hold a candle to Georgey."

"Georgey," Nikki sighed. "Do you think he liked our pics?"

Bennie Sue really wanted to know who Georgey was and what pics, but she was afraid to ask because she clearly wasn't in on the deal.

"Here's Georgey," Beth Ann dug in her backpack then slid a dog-eared picture across to Bennie Sue who uttered a "wow" when she saw the handsome, shirtless young man with well developed pecs.

"He's a little older than the pizza delivery boy, as you can see," Beth Ann explained. "But I like the more mature look. Don't you?"

"Yeah," Bennie Sue agreed. "He looks like one of those male models. Where did you find him?"

"At the park," Tosha broke in. "We used to talk to him over by the slides at first. He said we were so good looking he was sure we were models. He wanted to know which agency we worked for. He even asked to see pics from our photo shoots. We told him we didn't even have a camera, and he brought us one the next week."

"So now we take our own pictures," Nikki added. "Beth Ann is really good. We give him the camera one week, and he gives it back to us the next. That way he knows what we're doing in our lives."

"Does he give you lots of pictures?"

"No, he said the last ones we took didn't come out right. But he'll give us some more later."

Bennie Sue checked the clock and began taking off her finery. She was very careful to get all the lipstick off this time. She absolutely loved being included in a Friday party, and she didn't want to hack Della off.

7

The four girls continued to play together after school on Fridays. Sometimes they went for long bike rides over to Spadra creek. Sometimes they visited the University of the Ozarks campus where they imagined that they, too, were grown up. About every two weeks, they had a party at Beth Ann's.

One Friday, the power went out at school around 2:00, and classes were dismissed. The kids were supposed to contact parents, but not all of them did, including Bennie Sue.

"Let's go to your place today," Beth Ann suggested. We never go there. Besides I've been dying to see your mother's Jacuzzi. Is it big enough for all of us?"

After being in Beth Ann's house, Bennie Sue dreaded taking the Three Musketeers to her little mobile home. She just knew they'd make fun of her. But at least she had a Jacuzzi, and the others didn't. The other three inspected the mobile home thoroughly. Beth Ann even opened drawers and cabinets looking to see what she might find useful. Then they headed for Della's bedroom and bathroom.

Here the Three Musketeers, following Beth Ann's lead, looked in the drawers and fingered Della's jewelry and cosmetics. Now for the bathroom!

Bennie Sue showed them how to fill the tub and turn on the jets. Then she poured a little bubble bath in. The girls smiled when they saw the bubbles forming. Then Beth Ann grabbed the soap bottle and poured about half of it in. The bubbles rose up like snow and kept rising until they were sliding over the top of the tub. Bennie Sue began grabbing towels to wipe them up from the floor. Meanwhile she turned the water off. If the tub overflowed, Della would punish her severely.

The other three were oblivious to Bennie Sue's panic. They stripped off and jumped into the tub with its lovely bubbles, grabbing huge handfuls of them and throwing them at each other. "Stop! You've got to stop. My mom will kill me!" Bennie Sue begged.

"Chill out, little girl," Beth Ann insisted. "We'll help you clean up (the other two nodded their agreement). Right now we just want to have some fun. Now where's my camera? We've got to make some pictures for Georgey." The other two giggled at the prospect of pictures in the bubbly water, just like the advertisements on TV.

When one of the other nurses on her floor mentioned that the power was out at school, Della became concerned. Why hadn't Bennie Sue called her? One of their rules was that they would stay in contact if anything changed in their schedules.

Della talked to the charge nurse and signed out a half hour early, headed for home.

Della turned into her driveway and saw four girl's bikes on the grass beside the front doorstep. Not sure and parentally suspicious of what the girls might be up to, she turned the knob on the unlocked front door very slowly, opening the door just enough to peek in. They weren't in the front bedroom or living room. She could hear peals of laughter coming from the back bedroom.

Della froze in place when she reached the bathroom. Three naked little girls were sitting on the edge of the tub with mounds of bubbles placed over their pubic areas and nipples, mermaid style. They were posing suggestively for the camera which was being operated by Della's own naked little strumpet!

"Take another one," Beth Ann instructed. "We want to look really sexy for Georgey."

"What are you doing?" Della screeched. Eight pairs of eyes suddenly turned toward her. Tosha and Nikki covered their mouths in surprise. Beth Ann frowned as if to say, 'What's your problem, lady?' and Bennie Sue grabbed a soggy towel to cover herself.

"Give me that!" Della snatched the camera from Bennie Sue. "Who's Georgey?"

"You know, Georgey, Porgey, puddin' and pie," Beth Ann was exasperated with this dense adult.

"Well, you little puddin's get your clothes on!" There was no question that she meant it. Della was appalled. She knew instinctively what she was dealing with. She was not going to let this happen to Bennie Sue. Not again. While the girls were getting dressed, she grabbed the phonebook and looked up the number for the local police. "I have four little girls here with me who appear to be involved with a pedophile. What should I do?" She silently prayed that what ever this mess turned out to be, Bennie Sue would not be further damaged.

"Are you their parent?" came the voice of a man, presumably an investigator.

"I am the mother of one of the girls. I do not know the other parents."

"Wait right there (he took her address and phone number). We'll send someone over there to get some of this straightened out. Don't let anyone leave until we get there."

Pedophiles rated high priority in the counties of the River Valley.

The girls were very uncomfortable. When they were dressed, Della sat them down at the kitchen table, but didn't say a word to them. She had no intention of being a go-between for children she barely knew. Let their own parents shoulder that task!

In less than 15 minutes a plain clothes investigator and a female officer in uniform were knocking at the door. Della had literally been barring the door to block Beth Ann, Tosha and Nikki who had suddenly decided they needed to go home because their mothers were expecting them. Della remembered the old rule: If your friend's mother gets upset with something you and your friend did or didn't do, leave!

They ended up with Detective Cash's and Officer Streeter's taking the Three Musketeers to the police station where they would call their parents. The detective also took the confiscated camera with him to get prints made. The police were not about to question the threesome unless their parents were there, and preferably not until they knew what was in the camera. Della agreed to take Bennie Sue with her to pick up Cheyenne then meet the officers at the Clarksville Police Department (CPD).

8

Della and the girls were met at the CPD by Officer Streeter who led them to a common lounge area with a coffee pot and various snack machines. "It's going to be a while," she apologized. "Detective Cash had to take the camera out to Jerry's Camera to get prints. It's a Canon Power Shot, and it hasn't been out very long, and we don't have the equipment to print from it. Besides, a Canon printer's a little too pricey for our budget right now."

Fortunately, after her experience with her ex-husband's arrest, Della had known all about "hurry up and wait". She had taken a little extra time gathering a few toys for Cheyenne and books for herself and Bennie Sue. Nevertheless, their heads bobbed up every time someone new came through the front door. Detective Cash finally emerged from a back hallway after nearly two hours. He nodded at her and motioned for her to follow him. He pushed out his palm indicating Bennie Sue should stay with the toddler.

"Ms. Webb," he began after they were seated and the door was closed, "I'm sorry to do this, but I need you to look at some pictures." He handed her a photo envelope and watched while she looked through the pictures.

Talk about shock! There was only one picture of Bennie Sue sitting in the Jacuzzi with bubbles up to her armpits, but the other three were dominantly pictured alone or in twos, since one of them had to act as the photographer. There were a total of 12 photos, including the one Bennie Sue was taking when Della caught the girls. The photos were clearly intended to be sexy. Most of them were explicitly revealing. One of them even showed two of them from the back, bent over with their little naked cheeks spread to show their anuses!

Leaning an elbow on the arm of her chair, Della dropped her forehead into her open hand and slowly shook her head as if in denial. However, when she raised her head and looked at the detective, she was in full control. "What can I do to help stop this?"

—⚹—

That night seemed endless. Detective Cash interviewed Bennie Sue first since the other parents hadn't arrived yet. Unfortunately, as the fourth wheel of the triad, she had very little specific information. She knew the other three had a friend named Georgey who liked to look at their pictures. She had never seen him, but Beth Ann had a picture of him in her backpack. Georgey was an "older man" who was very handsome. Sometimes Beth Ann took pictures when the foursome were together, but today was the first day Bennie Sue had been asked to take pictures. She further revealed that when the girls had parties at Beth Ann's, her mother was out shopping. In fact she had never met the woman.

Della was allowed to take her girls with her until she found a place for Cheyenne to spend the night. She and Bennie Sue would get some supper while they were out then return to the CPD. Meanwhile Detective Cash would wait for the other parents then question each girl with a parent present. He might want to question all of them as a group, so Della and Bennie Sue needed to return.

Detective Cash would like to have questioned the ring leader, Beth Ann, next, but her parents had not arrived. Tosha's and Nikki's mothers were sitting together sharing misinformation, and Cash needed to break that up. Nikki told him the girls had met an older man in the park near the merry-go-round. They had been spinning each other trying to go faster and faster. The man they called Georgey had offered to spin all three of them at once. It was great fun. After that, they saw him often, and sometimes they'd ride their bikes around the park looking for him.

Tosha filled in that Georgey thought they were models and had asked them which agency they worked for. He said he knew someone from an agency and offered to take some shots of them.

When his friend at the agency said he liked the girls, but needed a lot more pics, Georgey had given a camera to Beth Ann. He said he needed natural shots. Beth Ann would take a week's worth of photos; then they'd bring the camera back to Georgey. They'd usually skip a week before he brought the camera back.

When the two mothers saw this week's pictures, they were first amused, then horrified. The girls had been very busy shooting pictures for Georgey!

Della and Bennie Sue returned to find Tosha and Nikki sitting with their mothers on opposite sides of the room. Beth Ann was alone in a big overstuffed chair reading a book. Della and Bennie Sue sat on a couch together in the middle of the room while they waited for at least one of Beth Ann's parents to show up. From the looks on the other two women's faces, Della knew they had seen the photos. They looked like relatives at the hospital, "holding up", wondering if their patient was going to be all right.

Finally, at about 5:30, Beth Ann's father appeared. He was wearing tweedish dress pants and nice shoes. His shirt was open at the collar and covered by a loose fitting jacket. His hair was neatly cut, and his demeanor was positive. Salesman! Della pegged him immediately. She was prepared to dislike him since he had been keeping all of them waiting, but she found she really wasn't angry with him now that she had seen him.

As Beth Ann and her father were directed to the interview room, Detective Cash sent Beth Ann back to retrieve her backpack. He remembered Bennie Sue's statement that Beth Ann had a picture of Georgie. Beth Ann's father apologized profusely for his late arrival. He had been helping a client file an insurance claim. Beth Ann's mother couldn't come because she was up in the air somewhere. As a flight attendant based out of XNA, she was gone a lot. The detective explained briefly to the father, as he had to the mothers, that Beth Ann and her friends had apparently been taking "candid" pictures of themselves to be given to a man called Georgey. He called Officer Streeter in to witness the interview.

Beth Ann was a babble of information. Nine, going on 30, she laid it all out. Yes, they had met Georgey at the park. And yes, he had given her the camera to take pictures. He was compiling a portfolio for the three girls to present to an agent. He thought they had a bright future as child models. The agent had seen some of their pictures and had commented that the girls were too old to be babies and too young to be women. He said there was a good market now in tweens, but the girls needed to show a more sophisticated profile. He suggested they watch commercials on TV and try to reconstruct some of the ideas, like Victoria's Secret's sexy lingerie and naked people in bubble baths. That type of picture would be great for advertising to teens.

Beth Ann began rummaging through her backpack then slapped a photo onto the corner of the desk between her father and the detective. The sharp intake of air from her father signaled that he recognized the subject. "That's him," Beth Ann informed them. "Isn't he divine? That's our Georgey, or whatever his name is. Give me a break. No grown man calls himself Georgey! He had better have our portfolio or I'll keep the camera and kick him to the curb." Beth Ann's father was horrified to hear his daughter reciting lines as if she were in a soap opera that she was making up as she went.

"Aren't you afraid he might hurt you?" Detective Cash was concerned.

"Oh, no. If he bothers me, I'll just tell everyone he's a pedophile," Beth Ann smirked.

—⁂—

Officer Streeter escorted Beth Ann back to the waiting area where she smiled at the others like a fox in the chicken coop. Meanwhile Detective Cash was eager to talk to her dad. "You know who he is, don't you?"

"Yes, I do," he said flatly. "That's Seth Gunter. His father is Carson Gunter. He's in real estate and insurance. He owns about half of Johnson County, and what he doesn't own, he insures. Seth works as an adjuster, when he works. He likes to spend his daddy's money, " there was disdain in his voice.

Detective Cash called the parents in and asked them if, since today was Wednesday, they could manage to keep the girls out of school for the next two days. He needed time to present his evidence to a judge and get search warrants for Seth Gunter's home, office and car. Hopefully CPD could pick him up this weekend. Meanwhile the less everyone talked, the better.

Della suggested that the girls could have a stomach virus. Since they ran around together, no one would suspect anything unusual if all of them had it. Tosh's mom offered to keep Beth Ann at their house while her dad worked. Nikki's mom and Della would arrange for their girls to stay with relatives.

9

Detective Cash spent the next two days trying to get all the ends tied down for a search warrant for Seth Gunter's house, car, and office. If they found what they suspected was there, an arrest for probable cause would follow. First he told the story to the Chief of Police who simply sat at his desk and shook his head. He was always amazed at the ingenuity of some criminals, and he had learned that in no way had he "seen everything".

They decided to go to Circuit Judge Collin Reston who was known to go hard on child sex offenders. But Judge Reston was sitting on a task force in Ozark this week and was expected to be out of town until Friday afternoon. The investigator and chief decided to wait. And, of course, Judge Reston didn't get back until after 8:00 Friday night. Members of the task force had persuaded him to stay a little longer to enjoy the first class bar-b-que at Riverfront Bar-B-Que.

Like the Chief of Police, Judge Reston just shook his head after the situation and supporting documents had been laid out for him. He sighed and signed the warrant. Seth Gunter had been thumbing his nose at the police for years. He was one of those young men who skated just on the edge of the law. He'd been accused of several offenses with underage girls, but with a good lawyer and Daddy's influence, he had never been arraigned. His dealings with these four little girls might be the smartest and the stupidest thing he had done so far.

Seth Gunter was awakened at 6:30 Saturday morning. The police descended on him in a small hive. He was politely asked to remain in the living room where he sat in his silk pajamas while his house and car were searched. On the outside, he appeared cool and detached, but inside he was horrified. He realized from the search warrant that the police were taking all his cameras and his computer and all his storage devices. There were several family photo albums in the house that were bagged up and inventoried. Clearly they were looking for photographic evidence of child pornography. Anything financial wouldn't require taking the cameras. Thank God Beth Ann still had the Power Shot. Didn't she?

After a thorough search of Gunter's house and home office, the team turned to the car and garage. Short of hidden cubbyholes in the walls, the garage was a bust. There were a few old tools and appliances on a workbench, but nothing in the overhead cabinets. The car produced nothing. Gunter was relieved that he had moved his stash of marijuana last night. If they'd been looking for drugs with a sniffing dog, he would have been sunk. But the probability was very low that they'd glom onto that old microwave over there on the bench with its control panel hanging out.

Beth Ann's photos (and a few of his own) were printed on Gunter's own Canon printer (he had a lot more money to spend on photographic equipment than the CPD). Then he picked out the few that really spoke to him and destroyed the others. He transferred the images to his IBM PC with a 10K hard disc, erasing the culls. The computer and hard drive were currently hidden away inside the shell of the giant, outdated microwave.

The search of Gunter's office was not fruitful. So, the CPD was left with the evidence they already had in hand. They had the Power Shot with one good fingerprint from Seth. They had the photos that Beth Ann and Bennie Sue had taken. And they had the girls' versions of their agreement with the man. Without additional evidence, they had a very weak case of he-said-she-said between a grown man and three (Bennie Sue had never seen him) highly impressionable little girls.

10

While the Three Musketeers and Seth Gunter were able to shrug off an unpleasant day, Bennie Sue encountered unintended consequences that would change her life forever. The legal system came back into her life. When a courtesy summary of the pedophile case from Johnson County crossed his desk, Pope County Circuit Judge, Clay Matthews, who had presided at James Blackwell's trial and who remembered the little girl who had testified just last fall, immediately became concerned and initiated an investigation of his own.

Bennie Sue's CASA volunteer, who had seen her a month ago, reported that Bennie Sue was adjusting well in her new school and was making friends. The principal at her school talked to her teachers who said that her grades were solid and that she had begun participating in classroom activities. They reported that she had been taken in by three of the most popular girls in the lower elementary school. Detective Cash said that Bennie Sue was an innocent who had been scooped up by three more sophisticated girls, one in particular, who were being groomed by a pedophile. Judge Matthews ordered a psychiatric evaluation. The court was for-tunate to have recently added a young psychologist who had worked with Child Protective Services in Dallas County, Texas. Judge Matthews had one of his minions call Della Webb to schedule a session for Bennie Sue with Dr. Michael Dintleman.

Della was not a happy camper. She remembered Michael Dintleman from some of the wild fraternity parties she had attended at Mt. Nebo State University (MNSU). How could she complain that she didn't trust him when he could make the same complaint about her? If the judge found out how wild some of those parties had really been, and that Della and Michael had been sexual partners from time to time, he might throw both of them out of court! Better to keep things calm and quiet for her daughter's sake.

Michael remembered the name, Della Webb. He thought he had met her at one of the Tau Tau Tau frat parties years ago, but his heart skipped a beat when he saw her in person. He had actually had sex with this woman! He started breathing calmly and slowly, displaying absolute professionalism on the outside. Della also appeared to be perfectly calm. Water under the bridge and all that. Her years as a hospital nurse, which required total discretion, served her well.

"Uh," he said, " If you want me to recuse myself, that is if you're uncomfortable with this…"

Della took a deep breath. "No, it's OK. That was a long time ago, and besides, it's not related to this situation at all."

Alone with him in a consulting room before Michael talked to Bennie Sue, Della told him her sad story as briefly as possible. Last fall, during the trial and subsequent divorce, her old family minister, Brother Samuels, had advised her well. He told her that people were going to be leery of her, being afraid that her "affliction" was contagious. They would nevertheless be fascinated by her experience and dig for details. "You need to decide what you are willing to tell people, what your story is. It does not have to be the complete story. Something simple will work quite well. After you repeat it several times it will seem like a normal thing to say."

Della's mantra had become, "He sexually abused our daughter and showed her child pornography. He is now in prison, and I had to divorce him to make sure he could never come back." She had learned to recognize other people's mantras when she heard them: "We just grew apart, but we're still friends." "He needed more space to find himself." "He's/she's not the person I married." "He/she had a little something on the side." "I got a good job offer, but he/she wouldn't leave his/her mother." And, one of Della's favorites, "He said I was keeping him from being the kind of Christian he wanted to be."

Della and Dr. Dintleman discussed reasonable options for Bennie Sue. She could be left alone in place. The school situation had once again turned scary for her. The kids were teasing her about taking striptease pictures, and the Three Musketeers were shunning her as if they didn't even know her. The remaining two months of this year were going to be a hard go. Perhaps the school could help separate her from the Three Musketeers. She had started kindergarten at five-½ and was now in the third grade. The school had two fourth grade classrooms, so that option was feasible, but not until next year.

Della admitted that she simply didn't have the resources to move again, or the energy to set up transportation outside the school district. Della's sister, Alexis had offered to take her. She lived in and taught third grade at Pottsville. That would be close enough for Della to see her daughter frequently, but she felt that she, and she alone, should raise Bennie Sue. She never wanted Bennie Sue to think she had been abandoned by both her parents.

Sitting outside the small interview room while Bennie Sue talked to Dr. Dintleman, Della thought about what her minister had said, "Don't pretend things are 'just fine' or that lots of people have it worse than you do. Something really bad has happened in your life, and this is a really hard time for you. If you can see forward to just a year, things will look a lot different."

Yes, she thought, *things do look a lot different, but they don't look very damn good. He got that part wrong. There's a pedophile out there running loose, probably with photos of my daughter. And now I have to deal with Michael Dintleman in my life. What did I do to deserve this?*

Dr. Dintleman told Bennie Sue to call him Dr. Mike. He wanted to be less threatening to the little girl, but he knew that children, especially those who had been abused, or those who had lost a father, had a hard time drawing lines with familiarity. They chatted about things at home and school. He soon recognized a pattern. Every question led to a dead end. She liked school, but she was afraid she wouldn't have any friends ever again. She loved her bicycle, but she was sure Della wasn't going to let her ride it to school any more. She loved her little sister, but she didn't know if it was going to be all right to take her beyond their tiny yard; someone might grab them. While Della, herself, had not seemed to be paranoid, clearly she had communicated fear of the present and a hopelessness for the future to her young daughter.

Bennie Sue felt safe with Dr. Mike. She wished somehow that he could be her father. Maybe he would ask Momma out.

Realizing that there were still two months of school, Judge Matthews asked Dr. Dintleman for a two-day turn around on his report. After reading Michael's findings and recommendations, he convened a late afternoon meeting with Della, Bennie

Sue, Alexis, and the CASA volunteer. Alexis's willingness to take Bennie Sue had been an important factor that tipped the scale. The Judge surprised them all by ordering that Bennie Sue be taken to live with Aunt Alexis by the end of the upcoming weekend!

He explained his ruling very patiently and very gently. Wherever Bennie Sue went to school, she would be the odd man out. In the Clarksville system, she was likely to be hassled, through no fault of her own. If she stayed at Clarksville, the next best window for adjustment would be in the fourth grade this fall. If she went with Alexis now, she could be placed into her aunt's class where she would be protected, and she could begin to make friends which might help alleviate an otherwise isolated and lonely summer. Most importantly, Bennie Sue was showing signs of PTSD. She had been through a lot in the last year, and leaving her where she was now might make it worse. No solution was guaranteed to make things "all better".

Judge Matthews emphasized that he was not casting any blame whatsoever on Della. In fact he suspected that she was experiencing some PTSD herself. Not having Bennie Sue to worry about on a daily basis could only serve to relieve her of some undeserved stress. Further, he felt it would be good for Bennie Sue to be out of the unspoken, but nevertheless sexually tainted situation. No child should be made to feel ashamed for an adult's bad behavior.

The order was temporary, only six months. At that time a review of the situation would occur. Meanwhile the two sisters would have joint custody, and Della would have full visitation rights. Della would pay $120.00 monthly to the court to be used by Alexis for Bennie Sue.

—⚶—

Bennie Sue was in a daze. Things that would affect her life were happening so fast that she had hardly any understanding of the enormity of the judge's order. She loved Aunt Alexis and always felt safe with her. And having her aunt as a teacher was way beyond cool. She also loved her mother and didn't want to disappoint her any more than she had already done. She could hear Della crying at night through the thin trailer walls. The adults didn't talk to her very much, and she was confused about what was happening. Cheyenne sensed the tension and became more demanding than usual. Taking care of the toddler's needs occupied a good bit of Bennie Sue's time.

During the next week, Cheyenne went to daycare as usual, and Della and Bennie Sue made several trips to Pottsville, mostly to the elementary school to get Bennie Sue enrolled. They had lunch with Aunt Alexis one day in the school cafetorium. The kids stared at Bennie Sue and whispered behind their hands. She desperately hoped some of them would like her.

Saturday came, and Della loaded up her little car with most of Bennie Sue's belongings. Since The girl would be riding to and from school with her aunt for the time being, the bicycle and CD player could wait until next week. Della was secretly relieved, knowing that Bennie Sue would be safe with Alexis. She was well aware that the pedophile who had been grooming the girls was still living in Clarksville.

Before they left the trailer, Della presented her daughter with a large package. Bennie Sue tore open the paper and smiled widely. She pulled the stuffed puppy into her arms, burying her cheek in the soft synthetic fur and hugging it tightly. She named the puppy Billy Bob, and for years she felt safer when she hugged him and thought of her mother.

Sixteen Years Later

11

Oh! Blessed Sunshine! It would be dark in about half an hour, and Bennie Sue wanted to catch every last ray this Thursday evening as she sat on her little deck polishing her toenails. A person can make a statement with finger nail and toenail polish. The bright red, sparkly polish said, "I am very sexy." Bennie Sue had a date coming up Saturday night. She hadn't been dating very much lately, and her date might never even see her toes, but she would know what rested below the surface.

Bennie Sue had been on-again/off-again with dating. Her experiences were mixed, and she was still a little insecure. Did the guy really want to get to know her, or was he just trying to get into her panties? She had a counseling appointment with Dr. Dintleman tomorrow afternoon. She'd hash it out with him again.

Bennie Sue had done some group dating where the kids usually paired off and held hands and snuggled or kissed, but she hadn't participated very much. Her first real experience with a guy of her own happened when she was 13. One of her friend's boyfriend had a cousin who needed a girl to go out with on a Saturday night. It was fall, and a group of students were going on a hayride. As the tractor wandered down dimly lit country roads, most of the couples started making out, some of them aggressively with full body contact and French kissing. Bennie Sue was a little embarrassed, but she let the cousin pull her down beside him in the hay. They had been kissing for a while when she told him that was very nice. He immediately rolled on top of her and said, "What's really nice is to rub those mountains on your chest and between your legs." Bennie Sue pushed him off her and hastily sat up. No one had ever said anything like that to her before! He kept trying to coax her back down into the hay, but she was resolute. She didn't care what the others did. This was not for her! When the cousin kept griping about what a lame date she turned out to be, she clammed up and thought to herself, *Tough Titties, so to speak*.

Bennie Sue really wanted to date when she was 15 and a sophomore. But nobody asked her. The couples at school were seriously entangled and already talking about getting married. Bennie Sue envied the popular kids who changed partners in what seemed like six-week cycles and started the whole drill over. She was somewhat cautious when she remembered her encounter with the Three Musketeers. Those very popular girls were into some things they should have let alone.

Well into her junior year, she was invited to a movie by one of the senior boys. Kevin was smart and funny and a little overweight. He wasn't bad looking, but he wasn't in the top tier of sought after guys. They hit it off and became classic "High School Sweethearts". In the spring, just before the prom, Kevin took Bennie Sue with him to visit the campus at the University of Central Arkansas (UCA). While they wandered around campus holding hands, Bennie Sue got an eyeful of public displays of affection. It was warm enough that couples were on spread blankets all over the place. Bennie Sue doubted that very much studying was actually happening.

It was when Kevin was a freshman at UCA and Bennie Sue was still a senior in high school that her inner conflict about sexuality arose. Kevin wanted more, and she wasn't sure she did. Sure she loved Kevin. And sure they were talking about getting married. But she still carried a sense within herself that sex was somehow dirty.

When Bennie Sue started college at Mt. Nebo State University in Dardanelle, AR, she and Kevin broke up. It didn't take him long to find himself a new girlfriend, and she was becoming involved in campus activities. It was in her anatomy class with Dr. Daniels that she heard some advice that made sense to her. Dr. Daniels pointed out that about 50% of students had had sexual relations before coming to the university. That meant that 50% had not. Further, by graduation about 80% of students had participated in sex, meaning that 20% had not. Her advice was very simple. Don't let anyone pressure you into sex because that person does not have your best interest at heart, and you are likely to get hurt. As long as you have sex only with someone who has your best interest at heart, you will do well.

Saturday night's planned date was with a college friend, Jeff Rose. They had toughed it out as lab partners in several chemistry and biology classes. After graduation Bennie Sue had gone to Little Rock to study forensic technology at the medical school on the recommendation of her mentor, Dr. Garnet Daniels. Jeff had gone to UCA in Conway to begin his studies toward a doctorate in physical therapy. They had kept in touch and went out for a movie or dinner from time to time.

12

Friday morning, Dr. Garnet Daniels, member of the Anatomy Department at MNSU, sat at her desk with a fresh cup of coffee from a pod machine perusing Russellville's daily paper. She had grabbed it from the box outside her house in Russellville as she headed toward Dardanelle for her morning anatomy class. This morning the paper was featuring the Ten Most Wanted criminals from neighboring Clarksville. As Garnet looked at their faces, a red flag went up. She reached for the phone and called the Clarksville Police Department.

"This is Dr. Garnet Daniels over at MNSU", she started. "I have some information about one of your Top Ten Most Wanted people."

"Oh, OK," the dispatcher/receptionist was very polite. "You need to talk to Tom Bradley. Tom's out on a call right now. Let me get your information, and I'll have him call you back."

Garnet was tempted to ask just how badly wanted these Top Ten people were, but she pulled it in and repeated her name and phone number. The small police departments around here were badly short-staffed and often fragmented. If she talked to someone besides Tom Bradley, he might not ever get the whole story.

Garnet took care of some paper work and reviewed the blood vessels of the thoracic cage for this afternoon's dissection. She had just enough time to run by the pharmacy before her early lunch with friends. Wouldn't you know it, as she reached for her purse, the phone rang. It was Tom Bradley.

She thanked him for calling back, even though she was the one with the information. The frequent overkill of politeness in this area of the country often smoothed the way for serious business. "I had Seth Gunter in my class last semester," she explained. "He said he wanted to be a Physical Therapy Assistant, but he didn't track right. He missed way too many classes, and when he was supposed to be in lab, he kept taking breaks to go outside to talk on his phone (we don't allow phones in the lab). The funny thing was that he withdrew about a week and a half before finals. He said he'd missed too much, which he had, and he would pick it up at UCA. He said he had found an apartment he could afford, so he better move over there while he could. Does that make any sense?"

"Oh, yes," he responded. "That would have been just about the time when we were getting ready to pull him in. He's one slippery character. He stays in one place just long enough to set up a small network of perverts. He deals in kiddy porn and seems to have plenty of money, so of course, we're looking for his 'clients' too."

"I'm sorry I can't give you more information. Maybe you can check out the Conway connection," Garnet said, finishing her end of the conversation.

"Yeah, we sure would like to talk to him. The Feds would too. Thank you for your tip." They said a few more ritual polite phrases and ended the call.

Garnet skipped the pharmacy and went straight to lunch at the Riverside Grill on Front Street in Dardanelle where there was table service and a calming atmosphere along side the Arkansas River. Dr. Rachel Pachebelle, a forensic pathologist for the State, and Dr. Hattie West, Director of Forensic Studies at MNSU were seated and waiting along with Bennie Sue Webb, now a Certified Identity Technician (DNA, fingerprints, etc.) who worked at the Forensic Lab at MNSU. Garnet had recommended Bennie Sue for the position, and she was delighted when her young student had taken the job almost two years ago.

Hattie and Rachel were discussing a newspaper article about the possibility of another branch of the State Crime Lab's being opened in Northwest Arkansas. For years the only Crime Lab was in Little Rock. That lab had gotten so far behind that it could take up to two years to get an autopsy, and rape kits were backdated for years. The Lab lost its National accreditation several years back. After the Lab had revised procedures and had finally come back into compliance, mismanagement raised its ugly head again. According to newspaper reports, the lab received a test sample of DNA to process. But, someone in the lab sent the sample out to a subcontractor instead of having the State Crime Lab process it!

The Forensic Lab at MNSU had been established as a teaching lab. Hattie West taught courses and gave seminars and workshops for law officers in the western part of Arkansas. Because MNSU taught most of the first two years of medical school course-work, it was equipped with a full size morgue as part of the Donated Body Program for the State. It wasn't much of a stretch to add a Forensic Pathologist (Medical Examiner) to the Forensic Lab to make it fully functional. Then the lab required a Certified Identity Specialist to log in and maintain the chain of evidence for legal proceedings. Bennie Sue Webb had been at the Lab almost two years now.

"Speaking of newspaper articles," Garnet asked, "did any of you see the Ten Most Wanted list from Clarksville this morning?"

They shook their heads, and she continued. "Well, I actually had one of them as a student last semester!" She had their rapt attention now. "So I talked to an officer in Clarksville, and he told me this kid is wanted for kiddy porn." Garnet noticed that Bennie Sue winced and closed her eyes for a few seconds. The close group of women knew what had happened to Bennie Sue. Their agreement was to talk about it only if Bennie Sue started the conversation.

"I remembered that he said he was moving to Conway at the end of semester. I don't know if that will help or not. There's really no telling where he's slithered off to." Bennie Sue smiled and nodded her head, agreeing with the characterization.

The women didn't linger today since they all had classes and appointments. Garnet left first so she could swing by the pharmacy as she had planned to do earlier. Hattie and Rachel were trying to schedule summer workshops already. And Bennie Sue planned to run a few more rape kits that had been sent up by the State Crime Lab in Little Rock before her 4:00 counseling appointment.

Bennie Sue had been seeing Dr. Michael Dintleman for a year and a half now. Since that fateful summer when she moved in with Aunt Alexis, Bennie Sue had gradually come to understand how wise his recommendation was. So, when she returned to the River Valley as a working adult, she sought him out. She thought she had worked through most of her issues with her past, but she still needed to talk to a therapist from time to time. Dr. Dintleman taught at MNSU and ran a private practice out of his home office. He lived out of town a few miles, and the drive helped Bennie Sue make the transition from work to self-evaluation.

Dr. Dintleman was helping Bennie Sue work through her sense of guilt regarding isolation from her mother, Della. When Bennie Sue was moved to live with Aunt Alexis 16 years ago, Della had expressed a desire to have Bennie Sue back with her. However, as time progressed, Della had become involved with a series of men who replaced her need for contact with Bennie Sue. Bennie Sue ended up staying with her aunt, and her visits with Della lagged until they became almost nonexistent. Then Bennie Sue was gone for almost two years, living in Little Rock while she finished her classes and internship to become a Certified Identity Technician. She had seen Della only at Christmas and the Fourth of July during those two years, and the relationship was clearly on hold.

She had made contact with her mother a few times since returning to the Valley, but she had not achieved the expected resolution. Her mother was not exactly hostile, but she wasn't very welcoming either. She still held Bennie Sue responsible for sending James Blackwell to prison, although she claimed she had moved on since then. And after she had been drinking, she allowed as to how he probably deserved it, especially after she found out he had another woman on the side. Since Momma was a born victim, it was hard for her to ever think of anyone, let alone a child, as a victim too. Dr. Dintleman had worked with Bennie Sue, teaching her to use cognitive therapy to recognize the distortions that led her to the unrealistic expectation that Momma would somehow welcome her back.

She had also begun to recognize the distortions in Momma's thinking that allowed her to think that the next man would be the answer to all her problems.

Bennie Sue's sense of community was changing too. She had begun to build solid ties to her work colleagues who assumed she was competent and encouraged her to learn more and to be more in her chosen field. Bennie Sue had even begun thinking about entering a doctoral program. And, quite importantly, seeing for herself that women could have a good relationship with a lover and/or a spouse had led Bennie to think about starting to date after all these years.

"I just can't seem to trust men, not about anything male-female anyway," she admitted.

"That's a distortion," Dr. Dintleman responded. "What kind?"

"Oh, crap! It's all-or-none. All men are the same, and therefore no man can be trusted," she answered.

"And what is a more realistic perception?" he prodded.

"Some men are guilty. Some don't want anything but sex. But, not all men are that way. The thing to do is to analyze the situation and look for red flags (and boy, do I know the flags). If there aren't any flags, then spend more time with the guy."

"Good," he continued. "Now look at the other assumption: if he wants sex, he has to be discarded."

"Yeah, I see. That's all-or-none again. I guess it's possible that some men might like me and want sex too."

"I think that's quite likely. You're a very attractive young lady, and," he paused for emphasis, "you are very well educated, and you have a fascinating career, and you become animated when you talk about your work. What's not to like? If you weren't my patient, I'd be asking you out myself."

Her eyes widened at this last piece of information. Dating Dr. Dintleman? He was almost old enough to be her father. Still, he was very handsome, and very well educated, and had a fascinating career, and... The idea of an older man had never really occurred to her.

"OK, I'll lighten up," she offered. "I'll have to remind myself that a date is just a date. It's not an appointment for sex, and I still have control."

They chatted about work for a while, and she made an appointment for next month. Maybe, she told herself, she'd try some of that male-female stuff in the mean time.

As Bennie was backing out of the parking area for patients, another car was coming in. She admired the little white Nissan Juke with the red and black twisted racing scarf trim on the sides. Maybe she'd get one of those when she replaced her current heap.

—◊—

The Saturday night date was really fun for Bennie Sue. Jeff picked her up at 5:45, and they made it to the Golden Corral on Hwy 22E just ahead of the crowd. They both had half slices of rare beef with horseradish sauce and every kind of shrimp on the buffet. Bennie Sue picked sliced tomatoes and cukes while Jeff had a loaded baked potato. They both picked the fudge cake with whipped topping for dessert.

Bennie Sue had snagged tickets for an 8:00 showing of *Hacksaw Ridge* at the Student Center cinema, so they drove her car with a campus parking sticker. The movie's battle scenes were emotionally tense, and Bennie Sue found herself on the edge of her seat several times. During one scene she almost squeezed Jeff's hand off, holding on for support.

Afterward they went to Brahms for a shared banana split which they agreed neither of them needed after their earlier fudge cake dessert. Jeff managed to snag most of the banana while Bennie Sue scarffed up most of the chocolate sauce. For some reason they got off onto embarrassing situations, and Jeff repeated a story he had heard from one of his friends. Seems this fellow is out on a date when he has an attack of IBS. He rushes to the men's restroom and makes it on time. However, there's no toilet paper in the single stall. So he pulls out his cell phone and calls his mother who just happens to be shopping in the store next door. She races over and finds the manager and urges him to rush some toilet paper to the men's restroom.

Jeff had to be up early Sunday to take his grandmother to church, so they called it a night and drove back to his car. Before he left he came around to her window and gave her a long, sweet kiss. "See you in two weeks. My turf next time." She wiggled her red polished toes as she realized she was already looking forward to it.

13

Dr. Michael Dintleman, was having a particularly pleasant Sunday evening. He had just experienced wonderfully satisfying sex with Melissa Owens, one of his former students. They had showered, and she had dressed. She had just gone, and he was sitting in his favorite recliner, wrapped in a huge towel, enjoying a glass of a very good cabernet sauvignon. He checked the clock on the wall. Time to get dressed himself. Less than a half hour now until one of his current students, Emily Leonard, was coming by to drop off her term paper.

Michael would have liked very much to have sex with Emily. She fit his "type", long blonde hair, slender body, plenty of breast. But he knew better than to hit on a current student. He was saving her for next semester and looking forward to finishing the seduction that had already begun.

As he leaned back in his chair, savoring his wine, the front door opened. "Did you forget something?" he called to the person he assumed was Melissa. His voice was sweet, but, truthfully, he was a little irritated at her forgetfulness and the disturbance of his daydreams. He hurriedly sat up in his recliner, sloshing a small amount of wine onto his bamboo floor. It was not Melissa! It was a much larger person wearing a ski mask and carrying a baseball bat!

Michael's pupils enlarged as he sensed danger, and he struggled to fully right his recliner and get up. Too late! He threw up his arms in defense, and flailed at the attacker without managing to scratch through the long sleeves on his arms. But as the bat struck full force, the last words he heard were, "You're not going to take her away from me!"

The bat struck repeatedly with rage until Michael's empty eyes signaled that he was dead. The attacker pulled the bloodied towel from Michael's body, satisfied that his nakedness would be seen by others. Michael was not such a "big" man now. After rummaging in the bedroom, the murderer brought a used condom full of Michael's ejaculate and stuffed it up his anus with a pair of chopsticks from the kitchen with an angry vengeance. Then the attacker took a picture with a cell phone. The scene was too perfect to resist!

The murderer ransacked the house, going through all the filing cabinets and drawers, not just in Michael's home office, but in his bedroom and his kitchen. Unable to find the desired object, the attacker picked up the bat that had been lying in a pool of blood and quickly left the house.

—m—

Emily Leonard drove west from Dardanelle, having difficulty reading the street signs as darkness fell. She caught the sign for Bobcat Hollow just as she passed it, so she had to find a safe turn-around place and come back. She was excited about going out to Dr. Dintleman's house by herself. He had told her very plainly that he didn't date his current students. But, pretty soon she wouldn't be his student. And who knows what might happen then? He had been the one to suggest she bring the term paper to his office, not at the university, but at his house.

The road curved through trees then opened up into a wide cleared area. His house was one of the new ones on the left, and it was easy to find. She climbed out of her sexy little Miata and retrieved her tote with the sequined peacock on it. She had brought it instead of her usual purse, so along with the paper, it had her phone, Driver's license, and a little cash.

She rang the doorbell three times with no answer, so she pulled out her phone and called Dr. Dintleman, just in case he was out back, or maybe in the shower. She could see herself being there with him next semester. Finally she tried the door which was unlocked. She opened it cautiously and called out to him. Something struck her as odd, especially when she saw the small streak of blood on the bamboo entry way. When she looked into the living area, she saw that the big recliner sitting askew, with a limp hand dangling over the foot rest.

"Dr. Dintleman, Dr. Dintleman? Are you all right?" she came closer to the chair. Then she screamed and ran back outside sinking to her knees as she vomited over the side of the steps.

14

Detective Sergeant Sophia Calypso finished rinsing the brunette hair coloring down the sink and reached for a towel. Sophia was a natural redhead, but she had hidden it for the past 10 years, ever since Ronnie had left her and she had recreated herself as a serious law enforcement woman. She wrapped the towel around her head and twisted it into a turban before heading to the kitchen for her favorite sweet iced tea. Then the phone rang.

"Dang!" she said out loud. "I hate being on-call on weekends."

Karen, the dispatcher was talking faster than normal, "There's a girl out at Dr. Dintleman's off Bobcat Hollow. She thinks he's dead. She says it's really bad, but I don't know what that means. I told her to stay put and we'd send the police and an ambulance. You better get out there fast. His is the second house in that new addition on the left. It's 2820 Cougar Lane. OK?"

Sophia grabbed her keys and her gun and set them on the table by the front door. Fortunately she was almost fully dressed. She flung the towel off her head and ran to the bedroom for one of her Dardanelle Police T-shirts and a cap to cover her wet hair. In less than five minutes, she was on the road with lights and siren going full blast.

As other officers arrived, Sophia instructed them to seal off the crime scene. No one would be allowed inside unless she said so! It was too easy to compromise a crime scene like this one. Well-meaning, but untrained officers could compromise forensic evidence needed for conviction at a trial.

Sophia and one of the EMTs, Bob Maness, entered the house together while the second EMT checked to see that Emily was all right. "Holy shit! What the hell happened here?" Bob burst out. He hurried to the recliner where he checked for pulses, but it was clear to both of them that Dr. Dintleman was dead, bludgeoned to death.

Sophia closed her eyes and took a deep breath,. She could have uttered a few choice words herself, that is until she had started recreating herself. The crime scene was shocking, guaranteed to give you bad dreams. Experienced law enforcement and medical people had to learn to shut off parts of their brains in order to make it through such a hor-rific scene, although it would never be completely buried. The naked victim lay mostly prone with one arm dangling over the foot rest of the recliner. The back of his skull was bashed and bloody as were his arms, indicating some attempt at defense. The pair of chopsticks protruding from his rectum amid the feces released at death suggested an especially perverse motive for murder. Smeared blood, urine and leaked fluids all over the chair and floor spoke of overkill. It would be difficult to rule out a crime of passion.

Being careful not to contaminate the scene, Sophia and Bob slipped on booties and gloves and began to examine the adjoining rooms together. As she walked, Sophia called her dispatcher to ask for the coroner and a Crime Scene Unit (CSU). The bedroom and the home office had been ransacked. The drawers and closets had been emptied onto the floor. The same trashing had occurred in the kitchen and utility room. Only the small guest room had been spared. With this mess, there was no way to know what the murderer had been after.

—⚶—

Dewey Elkins had heard a car coming down the road not too long before Emily had passed by, going toward Dr. Dintleman's. He had quickly slipped across the grass and dried weeds, blending into the scruffy bushes beside the small creek where he stood still and waited. He had learned long ago that if he simply froze no one would notice him at night, even if the lights were aimed straight toward him; the human eye had not been designed for night vision. However motion could be a dead give away.

Dewey was one of the area's wanderers. People assumed he was homeless, but he wasn't, really. He had devised a very comfortable tent and lean-to farther up the creek where he could stay most of the year. When the winter was bitterly cold, he had a cozy backup, but he rarely stayed inside for very many nights. Tonight, the temperature wouldn't get much below 50 degrees, and he'd be snug as a bug in his down sleeping bag.

Dewey pulled his bicycle and little utility cart into the bushes so that the approaching lights wouldn't catch any reflection off the metal frames. He was returning from his biweekly trip into Dardanelle for food and fuel for his little propane cook stove. He wasn't hurting for money. He had a small monthly check from a retirement annuity that paid for most of his upkeep, and there was the trust from his mother's estate, but he preferred his own company.

To Dewey's surprise, the large SUV slowed as it approached him and pulled toward his side of the road. Even in his frozen position, Dewey was sure he was being spot-lighted, just like a scared deer. He held his breath as the driver opened his door half way and slung a large object out onto the creek bank practically at Dewey's feet. The door was closed, and the SUV roared on down the road toward the highway.

Dewey sighed in relief, waiting until the car was out of sight before he turned on his miner's light and approached the object. He was careful not to touch anything as he slowly circled the piece of wood. *Man, oh man, oh man!* he half muttered to himself. *What have we got here? Somebody's sure as hell done somebody wrong.*

Dewey suspected foul play. About half an hour later when the lights and sirens flew past his little creek down the road in the direction the big SUV had come from, he was sure. He knew better than to put his fingerprints on the bloodied ball bat, even though he really, really wanted to pick it up. Instead, he took his cart and supplies up the creek to his shelter and returned with just his mountain bike. Soon he was on the road in search of all the excitement.

By the time he reached Dr. Dintleman's house, yellow tape had been stretched around the perimeter. There being very few neighbors, only a small crowd of onlookers was gathered on the lawn. Dewey leaned his bike against a tree and approached the patrolman who was watching outside to ask to speak to the officer in charge.

"Detective Seargent Calypso is inside now," the young officer informed him curtly. "You'll have to wait until she comes out."

Dewey hadn't really expected anything else, but the curtness set his teeth on edge. "You will tell her Dewey Elkins is here and that I have some important information, won't you?" he asked with firmness in his voice.

"Yeah, yeah, sure thing. But you're still going to have to wait."

Dewey ambled back to the tree where he'd left his bike and slid down to the ground with his back to the trunk. Waiting was something he did with considerable expertise. He sensed that Michael was dead, and he used the time to start getting his mind around it.

—⁂—

It was almost an hour before Sophia came up for air. She desperately needed to step outside. She had trouble getting past the stench of death. The animal smell of blood, plus the odor of urine and feces that leaked when sphincters relaxed, made her nauseous. Thankfully, there were not many homicides in this part of the county, but there were shotgun blasts and knifings, and they all stank!

The small bunch of neighbors had gone home when the body was removed, so she told the officer on guard that he could go home too then headed for her car. She had just opened her door when she became aware of someone behind her. She whirled quickly and came face-to-face with Dewey. "Damn, you startled me!" she burst out.

"Sorry about that," Dewey responded, "but that young guy wasn't going to let me talk to you. His manners aren't too good. I guess he hasn't been working with you too long."

Sophia chuckled and held out her hand. "How you doin', Dewey?" she greeted an old acquaintance. "What can I help you with? Those Jackson boys botherin' you again?"

"Nah, nah, no trouble there since you chewed them a new asshole last time. It's about that." He signaled toward the open door.

"Oh," she suddenly became serious, "What about that?"

"There's something I think you ought ta see." He told her about the bloody baseball bat down by the creek.

"Well, I guess we better take a look. That just might be our murder weapon. And that would really be a break. You're sure you didn't touch it?"

He shook his head no, and she swung into action. She pulled Lane, the last investigator, out of the house and sealed the door. What they had would wait until tomorrow. They put Dewey's bike in the back of Lane's truck. Dewey rode with Sophia, and Lane followed back down to the creek. It didn't take long for Dewey to relocate the bat. Sophia and Lane both oohed and aahed as they directed their high-beam lights onto the deadly object nestled there in the grass, preparing to rot over the ensuing years.

Lane collected the bat into two evidence bags because of its length and sealed them at the center. He signed and dated the tape to verify the chain of evidence, noting the presence of the two witnesses.

When Lane was gone, Sylvia cautioned Dewey. "Don't talk to anybody about this. You know what the gossips will say when they hear it was you who found the weapon."

"Yeah, I know. They'll have me sneaking up there to Michael's to rob him of something expensive. I was in the house while he was in the sack, and he confronted me with the bat. You know the rest of it."

"Yes I do. And I know I'd better get fingerprints and DNA from you for your own protection. You got any finger prints up there at the house?"

"I'm pretty sure I do. It's been a spell since I was up there, but it's possible."

"Tell you what," she was thinking about tomorrow. "I'll be by here again in the morning. I can stop by here then and get your samples. I don't have any swabs on me right now. We used all of mine at the house. Would, say, 10:00 be all right?"

"Sure," he agreed. "Come on back to the camp. Wear your boots and watch out for snakes."

"I always watch out for snakes," she asserted meaningfully.

15

When Detective Seargent Calypso visited the crime scene early the next morning, most of the odor was gone. The body had been taken to the morgue at the School of Medicine Forensic Facility at MNSU on the eastern side of Dardanelle. Dr. Rachel Pachebelle, Arkansas's best known forensic pathologist, would perform the autopsy early in the week. Meanwhile the CSU team would gather additional information.

After the finger print team had finished, the CSU team searched for any evidence that might identify the murderer. Aside from a foot print in the spilled wine near the chair, they found very little. The footprint would have been formed as the killer stepped away from the scene, dipping one foot into the wine then pressing the print plus a few smudges onto the floor. The narrow trail of blood in the entry way was possibly from the murder weapon which Sophia had guessed, judging from the shape of the skull wounds, was a rounded cylinder of some kind. She now knew that in all likelihood, the murder weapon was the baseball bat

Dewey had found. However, at this time, the evidence was inconclusive.

The CSU team took their time sorting through the havoc in the nearby rooms, taking hundreds of pictures along the way. Interestingly, a single page had been torn from the doctor's appointment book. Friday's appointments were missing. A cell phone was found under the desk in the home office. A forensic specialist would examine it thoroughly at the Police Department. Patient files had been pulled from the file cabinet in the office. A few in the K-M section were lying on the floor along with several small-capacity thumb drives. Inspection of the remaining files revealed that each folder had its own thumb drive, probably with Dr. Dintleman's notes on each patient. The CSU team gathered up those from the floor along with the jumbled folders for closer inspection later.

Sophia was especially pleased when one of the techs let out a whoop and came out of the laundry room with a 16-gig thumb drive in a zip-lock bag. It was in the doctor's pants pocket in the laundry hamper. Could this be what the murderer was after? This unexpected find had potential to yield much needed information. On the other hand, it could just be photos from a fishing trip.

—⁓—

Sophia was glad that it was still early spring so that the weeds and brambles hadn't completely overtaken the creek bank where the bat had been found. She walked around the area slowly looking for other evidence that might have been discarded. Finding none, she made her way up the creek to a dense stand of trees where Dewey had built his camp.

He was waiting for her and motioned her to a rocking chair he had just unfolded. Then he pulled two bottles of cold water from his ice chest, handed one to her and settled in his own rocking chair.

"This is some setup you have here," she complimented him as she surveyed his camp site. His tent was stabilized by a wall of logs fastened to a tall pine, and an overhead tarp extending from the tent provided shade and a wind break.

"Yeah, I got her fixed up pretty good. Took me a while, but then all I had was time. And I hate to admit it, but it really was good therapy."

"Was that what the doctor ordered?" she asked, showing empathy.

"Yeah, when I came back from Afghanistan, I had enough PTSD for a whole platoon. Michael really helped me out. When things got rough, I'd walk up the road and talk to him. I just can't believe he's gone," he shook his head sadly.

"When was the last time you saw him?"

"Oh, it's been a month or two. I've been pretty busy since I started sleeping all night. I've been going over to the old house some and doing some repairs. The physical work is good for me. I walk a couple of miles every day or ride my bike into town. It's slow, but it's coming along."

"Do you know anyone who would want to kill him?"

"No, I don't, and that's a fact. He was plenty wild when he was in college, but that was over 20 years ago. He still had an eye for the girls, though. They were always running up and down the Hollow. Could be he screwed the wrong one."

"That's kind of what I was thinkin'," she agreed. "But you know they'll be comin' after you because of your history. Let me get your fingerprints and a DNA swab so we can eliminate you. It'll save us time from going through the military data base.

"Sure thing." He let her ink his fingers and take a cheek swab, knowing she'd be back as soon as the lab ran the DNA.

—⁂—

Bennie Sue was really bummed out about Dr. Dintleman's death. She had passed the transference stage of therapy some time ago and now considered him to be a friend. Because of her connection to him, she asked Hattie whether she should get someone else to run the series of tests she normally performed. Hattie paused to think about it then responded, "Yes I suppose that would be better. If we ever catch the perp, this will likely go to trial. And we don't want the defense to argue contamination or partiality on your part."

The documentation of Dr. Dintleman's identity was basically pro forma, but necessary nevertheless. The task was assigned to Steve Hoyle, a forensic technician in the lab. Steve and Hattie went to the morgue to get finger prints and tissue for a DNA sample. Dardanelle's CSU had already supplied several samples of blood from the scene. Steve would run those against the known DNA. He fully expected a full match, but the blood would tell its own story. He would also run DNA from a hair sample for comparison against other samples in the house.

Steve Hoyle was an excellent technician who rarely made a mistake. People around the lab often made the lame joke that everything had been run "According to Hoyle." Nevertheless, he had to question the results when he ran Dr. Dintleman's DNA profile through the State's identification program early Tuesday afternoon. DNA was now collected from anyone charged with a felony, and of course, anyone who died by homicide or suspicious death. All Crime Lab employees were also in the system to rule out possible cross contamination.

With the new lab equipment, DNA analysis could be done in about 24 hours. The Crime Labs were coming closer year by year to the speedy times seen on TV. Because he was second guessing himself, Steve took an extra day to rerun one of the DNA samples. The results had not changed. Steve grabbed his sheets of computer paper and made a bee-line to Hattie's office!

"Oh my," Hattie inhaled sharply when she saw the results. "You're sure?"

"Yeah, I couldn't believe it either, so I ran it twice at the risk of wasting supplies," Steve assured her.

"Well, it is what it is," Hattie hesitated. "Go get our girl."

When Steve came back with Bennie Sue, Hattie looked at her as if she didn't know where to begin. "Tell me again who your father is," she instructed.

"James Blackwell. My mother divorced him when he went to prison and changed all of us back to her maiden name, Webb." When asked, Bennie was honest about her personal history.

"Well," Hattie tilted her head to the side, "I have some good news and some bad news. The good news is that James Blackwell is not your father. The bad news is that your father was Michael Dintleman." She handed the DNA reports to Bennie Sue. Bennie Sue looked at the pages; then she looked at them again, an incredulous look appearing on her face.

"I don't understand," Bennie Sue was truly confused. "How can this be?"

"Steve ran it twice. There's no mistake," Hattie cut off the next line of questions. "I'm sorry, or at least I think I am. I don't have the answers. It looks to me as if you're going to have to have a long conversation with your mother."

16

Tension was high in the Crime Lab. There was a rush on the Dintleman case because forensics could provide good clues for law enforcement. Bennie Sue was running everything else besides the Dintleman evidence.

The blood from the bat matched the victim's. There were lots of smeared fingerprints on the bat with one or two complete ones, suggesting the murderer had worn gloves during the battering, but pulled them off when he got back into his SUV. There was no match for the prints in the data base. The used condom yielded just a few epithelial cells from an unknown female. There was no match for the DNA. Surprisingly, there were no sperm in the ejaculate inside the condom. The shoeprint in the wine was a size twelve Nike; good luck with that!

The thumb drive from the victim's pocket had his prints and those of one unidentified person. Again, no hits in the data base. Currently, the thumb drive, along with others from the crime scene were being examined in Dardanelle's own cyber lab. With the onslaught of computer facilitated crime, especially child pornography and cyber-stalking, most law enforcement agencies had added specialists in cyber crime.

The autopsy confirmed that the victim had died from blunt force trauma to the head, probably inflicted by the retrieved bat. The victim was otherwise a healthy forty-something male who had been vasectomized, explaining the lack of sperm in the condom.

The angle of the blows indicated that the victim was struck from above and from the victim's left. Considering that the victim had probably been seated in the now upright recliner, the attacker was thought to be tall, probably at least six feet based on the shoe print, and was most probably right handed.

When Sophia came by for a conference with the Forensic Lab team, she expressed her frustration that none of the physical evidence pointed to a particular person. This was not surprising considering how brutal the attack had been, with the added insult of the chopsticks up the victim's rectum. Almost certainly the murder had been an act of passion. But by whom? The missing page from the appointment book suggested a connection with someone who saw the doctor on Friday. How did they get a handle on that?

Bennie Sue, who had been allowed to "observe" the conference, spoke up in a tremulous voice, "I was there Friday at 4:00. There wasn't anybody else there when I got there. But another car pulled in when I was backing out."

All eyes turned to Bennie Sue. "Did you see who it was?" Sophia asked excitedly.

"No, I didn't see the driver. But it was a cute little Juke, white with black and red racing ribbons on the side."

"Well, that gives us some place to start. We've got a bunch of faceless people to hunt down. Maybe this will help."

17

Monday morning after the murder, the owner of the cute little Juke, Cassie Kelly, wife of local Dardanelle banker Keith Kelly and mother of Candace (Candie) Kelly, a five-year old beauty queen, was waiting nervously for a knock on the door. Keith had called from the bank first thing to report the murder. She was upset about Dr. Dintleman's death, especially since she had seen him just the Friday before. Cassie and Keith were having a "rough spot" in their marriage. The truth was that there had always been a rough spot in their marriage, but it was morphing into something ugly, and Cassie was desperate enough to swallow some of her pride and seek counseling.

Cassie assumed that the police would be interviewing all the doctor's clients, and she was nattering in her mind about what she might be asked and what she would be willing to tell them. There were a lot of things in her life that she intended to keep secret.

Meanwhile, she was busy sewing embroidered roses around the neckline of Candie's latest costume, a little pink bikini. Her little princess was scheduled to compete in this weekend's Pea Vine Festival in Memphis. A win there would qualify Candie for the Easter Bunny Festival in Nashville next month. The Easter Bunny Festival was a MUST for serious Little Miss contenders. It would get national attention, and the winner(s) would get a shot at TV commercials, and who knows what after that. Cassie held the little bikini top against her chest and smiled to herself as she imagined her own sweet little confection smiling and bowing to the judges just before she was crowned.

It wasn't just the pride of ownership. After all, how can you own a person, especially one as wonderful as Candie? Besides Cassie had sworn to herself that she would never own her child, not the way her parents had owned her and her sisters. She thought she was past it, but then the dreams had started again. She had hoped Dr. Dintleman could help her. But now he was dead, and she didn't know who to turn to.

Cassie pulled herself back from her downward spiraling thoughts, back to the business at hand. She used up the rest of the thread and rethreaded her needle. She stuck the needle into her pin cushion then took a break to check the web site for orders. Their web site, Candie Kisses, had been set up to showcase their own little darling, but pretty soon, mothers were emailing to ask Cassie where she found some of the costumes. Why give someone else the business? It didn't take long for the

Kellys to see a great business opportunity. Soon Candie Kisses was selling clothing and accessories for little girls all over the United States!

Cassie was really proud of their business. She did all the ordering herself. She had a really good eye for just the right balance of razzle-dazzle and sweet innocence that seemed to please judges everywhere. Most of her suppliers would ship overnight so that she, in turn, could ship within two working days. Cassie also knew that her customers would pay top dollar for her services, so the shipping charges didn't eat away the cash. And, she didn't have to purchase and hold a large inventory. More cash margin for her!

Keith had been a real doll from the beginning. He was not only a banker, but also a computer whiz. He took care of setting up all the sales links and encryption for credit card sales. He also took marvelous pictures of Candie modeling many of the little outfits (just not the ones she'd be wearing next). And, if sales were slow, he sent out mass emailings to attract new customers. He monitored the purchases, sales, and taxes and made sure she had plenty of prepaid credit cards for spot purchases whenever and wherever she was out and about.

Cassie's mind went back to Dr. Dintleman's death and her last session with him. Keith had been more and more distant lately. He came home and spent about an hour with Candie, playing and looking at pictures in her growing portfolio. Then he went to is home office and sat down at the computer until dinner. Then it was back to the computer, completely ignoring her. He had been like that until just before Candie was born. Sex was about the only thing they still shared, but it was becoming less and less frequent. He seemed to get his satisfaction from browsing on the computer. And, he would hide the screen if she entered the room. He even turned his desk toward the door so she wouldn't accidentally see what he was doing. *How paranoid is that?*

Cassie read enough advice columns and women's magazines that it didn't take her long to zero in on porn. But she couldn't bring herself to confront him, especially since she couldn't find any on his computer while he was at work. She noticed he kept a big thumb drive locked up most of the time. When she asked about it, he said it was bank business, and he had to keep tight security on it.

When Candie was born, everything changed. Keith was thrilled. He helped her with the baby, even changing dirty diapers and taking night shifts when she was fussy. He started paying more attention to Cassie again, telling her repeatedly how thankful he was for her gift of Candie. One of their favorite things to do together was to go shopping for the baby. Before long, they had more clothes than she could ever possibly wear, although Keith was determined to photograph the little girl in every new outfit.

Candie won her first Little Miss pageant when she was three. Cassie and Keith had carefully selected and modified her dress until they both thought it was perfect. Everyone said Candie's little dress was the prettiest on the stage. That was when the Candie Kisses website was born. Cassie was obsessed with the web site, and Keith was obsessed with their daughter.

Now that Candie was five, the distance between her parents was growing again. Keith would come through their door and walk right past Cassie without even acknowledging her. He would go straight to Candie's room and wrestle with her and have her try on new clothes and practice her poses. The thumb drive moved in and out of its locked drawer again.

Cassie became depressed and started having sleep disturbances. When she mentioned her mood change to Keith, he was not only unsympathetic, but also condescending. "It's up to you," he had informed her. "You can choose to be miserable, or you can choose to be happy. People who are depressed want to be depressed. Not me. When I feel blue, I get myself up and make myself happy. You can do it too."

The depression had deepened until Cassie wasn't even enjoying buying beautiful clothes for Candie. She had finally decided she needed outside help and had seen her family doctor. He prescribed an antidepressant and referred her to Dr. Dintleman for counseling. "Medicine is good," he had said. "but most people do better with some talk therapy added in. I think you'll like Michael. He's good at getting to the nub of the problem."

And Dr. Dintleman had been good. Over a period of four months, he had helped her to see that the main source of her pain was in her marriage. She honestly did not feel loved. For Cassie, the key to Keith's obsessive behavior was locked up on that thumb drive! And she had begun to obsess about finding out for herself just what was on it.

18

Keith Kelly was having an "off" day at the bank. He couldn't stop thinking about Michael Dintleman. The cops were really going to have a hard time finding the killer unless they found a lot of evidence or maybe a witness. He knew the area where Dintleman lived. He had actually been in the house while it was being built with a loan from his own bank. The area was sparsely populated; witnesses were unlikely.

Keith was ambivalent about Dintleman's murder. Dintleman had a reputation for cutting to the core; he wasn't one to coddle relapsers. Either you wanted to get better or you didn't. Keith knew from his own firsthand experience with the man.

Keith admitted to himself that he had a little problem (he called it a fetish) with pornography. He thought women were beautiful, and the sight of their naked bodies turned him on. When he had married Cassie, she was one hot momma, and their romps in bed were quite satisfactory. But Cassie had become pregnant during their first year. He WAS NOT attracted to pregnant women. Besides, she was too busy with baby clothes and decorating a nursery to pay enough attention to him. So, he had begun to sneak off to his study where he enjoyed looking at porn.

When Candie was born, Keith thought he was the happiest man alive! He doted on his daughter, carrying her with him every place he went outside of work whether she should be there or not. He photographed her constantly. He knew how to elicit the cutest smiles from her. She was a beautiful child and seemed to be everybody's sweetheart.

It was Keith's idea to start entering her in Little Miss contests at the area fairs when she was three. It didn't take much to convince Cassie who was also a big fan of their daughter. When Candie started winning and Cassie had suggested a clothing web site as a small at-home business, Keith was eager to help. During the past two years he had been the business manager and the photographer. He loved posing Candie for web site pictures. And if a few of his photos were a bit naughty, who cared? Nobody was ever going to see them. It was his very own little secret.

Six months ago, Keith had started to experience pangs of remorse. Everyone assumed his life was perfect: perfect job, perfect house, perfect wife, perfect child, etc. These things were true, but he still felt a hole in his psyche, something he wasn't used to. So, he had seen Dr. Dintleman for several weeks. They had quickly zeroed in on the porn. Keith would never reveal the child porn; he knew Dintleman was required to report it since it was strictly illegal. But he was very defensive about the adult porn which was entirely legal and entirely turned him on.

Dintleman had also wormed out of him that he had promised Cassie to give up the porn, but had been unable to do it. Cassie was showing signs of depression. And the more she withdrew from him, the more he needed his porn. And, of course, the more he needed his porn, the more she withdrew from him. Now Cassie was seeing Dintleman, unaware that Keith had seen him previously (some things were intended to be kept secret). Keith's biggest fear was that Dintleman would support her if she decided to leave, taking Candie with her. That was something Keith could not allow to happen. So in retrospect, he wasn't ambivalent. He was glad the good doctor was dead!

19

Sophia's week, which was usually hectic because of the nature of her job, turned even more frenetic now that she had a homicide investigation too. Her first order of forensic business, besides finger prints and DNA, was to identify the owner of the epithelial cells on the outside of the condom. It was too early to be specific, but her working guess was that a spurned lover might be involved in the murder. Sex and money were always worth looking at. Fortunately her right hand man, Donny, would be following up on Dintleman's financials, and the cyber team would be tearing his computer and smart-phone apart. Meanwhile, her job was to *cherchez la femme*.

Finding a dead professor had done nothing for Melissa Owens. The poor girl looked like road kill when she appeared for her 10:00 interview. Her face was swollen from crying, and her makeup looked just a little smeared, probably because the usually taught skin was slightly puffy today. Her hair was a give away too. Her blond streaked shoulder-length hair had definitely not been styled today. She had twisted it to the top of her head and wrapped it with a scrunchie so that the straight ends stuck out. Her clothes were neat and clean; her jeans had even been pressed. Her boots and purse were well made and probably expensive.

Sophia motioned for Melissa to sit down across from her in the visitor's chair and offered her coffee or juice from the little fridge in the corner under the printer. When they had both opened their packaged cranberry juice, Sophia began. There was no use trying to calm the young lady. It might take days for her to settle down. Melissa had been totally cooperative last night, and the goal was to verify and expand on her statements.

"How long had you known Dr. Dintleman?" She started with the easy stuff.

"Two years. I had him for freshman psych, and I'm in his Behavioral Statistics course now. I was planning to apply for a research assistant position for next year."

"And why were you driving out to his house last night?"

Melissa blushed, "I couldn't hand in my assignment on time because I had to take my mother to Conway to the eye doctor. He told me to come out last night."

"Is that all? Nothing besides turning in an assignment?"

Melissa blushed again, remembering her fantasies about becoming the newest member of what the students called "Dintleman's Harem".

"Was it common practice for students to drive out to his home to turn in papers?" Sophia asked pointedly.

"Oh, gosh, "I don't know," Melissa stammered. "It was my only time, I swear."

"So you were aware that other students were driving out to his home to turn in assignments? Or what else might they be doing out there at night?" Sophia was being very direct.

"I guess I'd better tell you. It can't hurt anybody now. Dr. Dintleman dated students from campus. Not from his courses," she was quick to defend him, "but from past courses. There were quite a few coeds. They are/were known as 'Dintleman's Harem'."

"And who was in this year's 'Harem' ?" Sophia pushed for information.

"I'm not sure. I know last semester it was Ashley Hughes, and I think he was seeing Emily Leonard this semester. There may be others. I'm not sure."

"He didn't stick with them very long did he?" Sophia was wondering if the pattern of loving and leaving might be important to the case.

"No, I guess not. But we all knew that, and I don't think anybody expected it to last very long."

"Then why do it?" Sophia knew that relationships that were intended to be just for now often became emotional sinkholes for at least one of the participants.

"For the prestige. If Dintleman picked you, that meant you were one of the top dogs in the

Psychology Department. Other professors were more likely to give you a break on essay questions."

—⁓⁓—

Shortly after Melissa left, Sophia gave her crew instructions to find Emily Leonard and bring her in as soon as possible. Then she headed for the Department of Psychology at MNSU to find out more about this "Harem". She met with the chair, Dr. Marvin Shockley whom Sophia recognized from local news articles, but was otherwise unfamiliar with. He was very helpful with general information about Dr. Dintleman's activities as a faculty member. When she asked about the rumors of sexual encounters with students, he became very evasive, signaling that this line of enquiry was a dead end. He gave her access to Dr. Dintleman's office with the proviso that nothing could be removed without a warrant. She had already requested a warrant, but decided to go have a look around anyway.

The office was small, but well organized, much as his home had been. The requisite diplomas were displayed on the institutional beige walls along with scenic pictures of Arkansas parks and trials. The overall effect was fairly bland and non-threatening.

Sophia put her gloves on then sat down in Dintleman's chair and turned from side to side, trying to get a feel for the office. She skipped the computer and associated hardware, knowing that her cyber team would be better able to hunt for pertinent information. Instead, she began searching his desk. The usual assorted notes and papers cluttered his work area, and she wrote down the phone numbers scribbled on the margins of his big desk calendar. There were several appointments written in for later this week and next. She'd need the help of the departmental secretary to decipher those. As she tugged on one of the drawers, a pretty coed rushed through the door, then realizing Sophia was there, began backing out hastily.

"Whoa, there," Sophia commanded. "It's all right. I won't bite. Come back here. I'm Detective Seargent Sophia Calypso from the Dardanelle Police Department. And you would be?"

"I'm Theresa Wells, Dr. Dintleman's graduate assistant," the student replied. Then as Sophia kept looking at her expectantly, she continued. "I heard about what happened Sunday night. This is the first time that his door has been open, and I was hoping I could get the exams from Psych 305 to hand back. Classes will be cancelled the rest of the week, and I know some of the students will want to know their test scores." Her lips began quivering, and she suddenly broke into tears. "It's all so awful," she sobbed. "He was so nice to everybody. Why would anyone want to do that to him?"

Sophia motioned toward the visitor's chair and pulled a tissue from the box on the corner of the desk. Even though she felt sorry for the student, it was her job to get as much information as she could.

"Were you dating him?" Sophia asked gently, hoping she had found the donor of the epithelial cells on the outside of the condom.

"Me? No!" Theresa looked horrified. "Dr Dintleman never dated any current students or anyone he worked with. It was a hard and fast rule."

"But he did date former students?" Sophia pushed for information.

"Oh yes, everyone knew that. He had a whole line of hopefuls. People said he was promiscuous, but he usually dated just one (or maybe two) each semester. He once told me he didn't have time for all the fluff, what with his research and all."

"And what was his research?" Sophia really wanted to know.

"Pornography. He had some theories, sorry, hypotheses," she corrected herself, "about what drew men, well mostly men, toward pornography."

Sophia's eyes widened in response. "Was his research approved of by MNSU?"

"Well, they kind of tried to pretend it wasn't happening. I don't know what they were going to do when he started publishing."

"Was he close?"

"I don't know. I think he was still collecting data. You'd have to talk to Dr. Russell. They were working together."

Sophia made a note then asked her next question. "Do you happen to know who he was dating this semester, or even last semester, for that matter?"

"Well, I don't know about last semester, but this semester it was Emily Leonard. She was in his class last spring."

Sophia thanked Theresa and wrote down her number for future contact. Then she helped her find the test papers and escorted her to the door. The desk was basically a no-go since it was locked. The key was probably already at the station, so Sophia moved on to her next objective, the Registrar's office. She hoped to get class schedules, emails, addresses, etc. for students in the Psychology degree program.

The Registrar was very polite, but very firm. Her office could not give out information about student addresses or schedules without a subpoena. University policy. There was an online listing of current students, but a password was required for access. She did, however, supply Sophia with a list of administrative offices and phone numbers. Evidently those folks were not protected by any privacy rules.

Sophia called the office of the Dean of Liberal Arts and was referred back to the Department Head. Instead of Dr. Shockley, his secretary picked up. She looked up Dr. Russell's schedule and told Sophia he was in class until 2:00 after which he had research time scheduled. According to the secretary, Dr. Russell did not make any appointments on his research days and could be very hard to catch. So Sophia called Dr. Russell's number and left a voice mail that she hoped to meet him at 2:00. By then she felt as if she had been riding around the University carousel enough for one morning, so she headed back toward town to pick up a fast lunch and check in at her office.

Back at the Dardanelle Police Center, Donny and the cyber team were slowly extracting bits of information, trying to start constructing a large puzzle that pointed to the murderer. Dintleman's computer did not have notes from individual sessions. Apparently he kept a separate thumb drive for each patient. Technicians were trying to match the drives that were found scattered on the floor with their folders. Unfortunately, the identity of patients whose folders and discs had been taken by the murderer was going to be very difficult to trace down.

As it turned out, the computer did have a mother load of potentially useful information. Dintleman had kept very complete billing records dating back two years. The last cycle was two weeks ago, complete with names, addresses, and dates of appointments. A cyber-tech began searching for the missing patients, especially any in the K-M group.

Dintleman's phone was not very useful in its current form. His directory of about 50 people contained first names only. A low level rookie was given the responsibility to call the numbers trying to get full names and addresses, relationship to the deceased, and to find out when he/she had last seen Dr. Dintleman. Meanwhile Sophia headed back to MNSU to try to catch Dr. Russell before he disappeared into his "research", whatever that was.

20

Sophia was just rounding the curve of the top step on the second floor when she saw a man who must be Dr. Russell locking, then stepping away from his office door. He was a tall man with a headful of curly sandy-brown hair and a full beard that showed a few wide streaks of gray. There was nothing professorly about his dress. He wore snug jeans (nice bum) and a tucked-in blue T-shirt printed with a clothes line of "Freudian slips".

"Hey, wait," she hollered at him, determined to stop him.

He paused dramatically with his keys in his outstretched hand as if to say, "Why should I?"

She hurried up to him and introduced herself, "I'm Detective Seargent Sophia Calypso from the Dardanelle Police. I'm investigating Dr. Dintleman's death. And I really need to talk to you!"

He pulled a face that said he was disgruntled, "Oh very well. I suppose you do. Well let's get it over with. What's another afternoon wasted? Who cares about research any way?" He unlocked his door and motioned her to a comfy overstuffed chair next to his desk.

"I do," she was very emphatic. "I need to know what you've been looking at in case it's related to his death."

He ran his right hand through his hair and seemed to be pondering a profound problem. "Oh," he said, looking at her as if for the first time. "I hadn't considered that. I just...I just thought it was probably something to do with his...err...love life."

"Yes," she responded flatly, "that is another possibility. What can you tell me about that, before we get started on the other?"

"Oh my," Dr. Russell ran his hand through his hair again, "that is a very big subject. I hardly know where to begin."

"Let me point you," Sophia said. "Was Dr. Dintleman sleeping with his students?"

"Yes and no," he responded. "Michael had a thing for young lovelies, but he was careful not to sleep with anyone who was currently one of his students."

"How many of his ex-students did he sleep with?"

"Oh, my, I really couldn't tell you. Michael and I didn't talk about his love life."

"Oh for pity's sake," she felt as if she had opened a can of worms and was pulling one out at a time. "Make a guess."

"Well, he had quite a reputation already when I came here. But my guess, based on the last five years, is three or four a year."

Sophia did the math. Up to 20 students in the last five years alone! "Were there any of them who had angry boyfriends or, possibly, husbands?"

"Yes," he said, "there were several."

"Can you tell me about them?" she pulled out another worm.

"Well, there was one in particular, Evelyn Goodson. That was one weird relationship."

"How so?" she prodded.

"Well, Evelyn was married when she took up with Michael. But, as they say, she was just a little bit pregnant. God knows who the father really was. She was in his office all the time, and they flirted shamelessly. It was embarrassing for the other students and the faculty. Then toward the end of the semester, she up and moves in with him. But she was still married. It didn't make sense."

Sophia was relieved that Dr. Russell had finally loosened up. She needed to hear the rest of this story. "And?" she prompted.

"Well, when the baby comes, she's still living with Dintleman, and she files for divorce from Goodson. So everybody thinks she's going to marry Dintleman. And Dintleman is mum about everything. Then when the divorce comes through, Evelyn runs off with a graduate student over in Anthropology, and they move to Atlanta. Go figure."

He slowly shook his head, indicating that he just didn't understand how it all happened.

Sophia changed the subject to his research with Dr. Dintleman. Dr. Russell quickly held up both hands, palms out, to stop her. "I really do have to go to Ft. Smith to pick up some data from one of our subjects. I promise (he crossed his heart) I'll talk to you later." He checked his watch then offered, "Can you meet me tonight at Simple Simons, say about 7:30? My treat."

Sophia was surprised by his offer, but she needed to find out as much as she could before the trail grew cold. She checked her schedule on her phone and agreed to meet him. Who knew what she'd learn?

She went back to the station and started the crew tracing down Evelyn Goodson, her current lover, and her ex-husband.

21

Later that night Sophia met Dr. Russell as arranged. They ordered a large supreme pizza and salads. Dr. Russell had a beer, but Sophia considered herself to be still on duty. Besides, she was running low on energy, and alcohol was really not such a good idea on top of her hectic day. Maybe later, when she got home.

To her relief, Dr. Russell was very open and forthcoming about his research project with Dr. Dintleman. They were interviewing a large number of men who admitted to using pornography (not against the law) to identify patterns of arousal, and to get as much information as possible about why pornography was often considered an acceptable substitute for the real thing. Dr. Dintleman did most of the interviewing (and counseling subjects if requested), while Dr. Russell did most of the coding and statistical analysis.

An important part of their research, which made it different from most other studies, was collection of as much porn from each subject as possible. Quite a few of the men had simply copied their porn onto sticks for them (in fact he had delivered a stick to Michael on Saturday and had picked up one from Van Buren today, hence the dinner meeting). The research team was particularly interested in hard copies of subjects' porn. "We take the photos and copy them, giving the subjects all new photos. Then we examine the original pictures carefully to see which photos show greater wear. By matching the favorite photos with subjects' questionnaires, we hope to learn more about why particular images are 'sexier' than others."

"If I had them, I'd be taking fingerprints off them. You know of course, that quite a few of these guys are into child pornography too?"

"Oh, yes," he admitted, "we're well aware of that. But we can't really go there, much as we would like to, because it's illegal, and we'd have to report it if we knew children were being abused. That's why," he continued, "almost all research into child pornography has been done with people who have already been caught."

"Yeah, I know," Sophia nodded. "What I'd really like to do is catch some of the smarter ones. Almost every sizeable police department in the U.S. has someone working cyber-crime trying to stop child abuse."

"Well, before you ask," he grinned at her, "you can't have any fingerprints. Our subjects have been promised that their identities will not be revealed according to our Human Subjects protocol, and those that went into counseling are protected by HIPPA besides."

"Very well," she agreed. "I know you're right, but I sure would like to run them through our fingerprint systems."

"What can you tell me about what happened to Michael?" he asked in a solemn voice.

"Sorry," she explained, "I'm in the same ethical bind as you. I can't release any information while the crime is still under investigation. We'll have a hell of a time as it is to stop leaks. You know how everybody likes to talk around here. And for some reason, a lot of people don't think talking to family qualifies as a leak."

21

Emily Leonard, the young lady whose epithelials were most likely on the outside of the condom found in Dr. Dintleman's bathroom, had been easy to find and had agreed to come in first thing Tuesday morning. The comparison between her interview and that of Melissa Owens was stark. Emily's face was perfectly made up with the requisite arched eyebrows and large, perfectly lined lips. If there had been any tears cried over Dr. Dintleman's death, not a trace remained.

Emily was accompanied by someone Sophia assumed was a boyfriend. He was smartly dressed in a sport coat over very expensive jeans with an open necked pink dress shirt and handsome alligator loafers. He might have been the president of his toney fraternity at MNSU, but it was clear who was the boss. Emily pointed him to a bank of empty chairs where he could wait while she attended to business.

The first thing out of the young lady's mouth was, "Do I need a lawyer? My father is a partner at Levy, Lester and Leonard in Springdale. He told me

I probably wouldn't need representation for preliminary questioning, but not to answer anything that made me think you were looking at me as a suspect. Are you?"

Sophia was taken aback, but she held her facial expression steady as she replied, "No. Not at this time." She wasn't about to tell this presumptive young lady that the evidence indicated that a person much larger than she was the likely culprit. Still, they couldn't rule out that a partner, probably not the preppie in the waiting room, might have done the job. The time line in this case had to have been very tight, possibly a window of less than 20 minutes. It was important to tie things down.

"What we need from you," Sophia continued, "is as narrow a time line as you can give us. If you'll stipulate (hopefully a better choice of words than concede) that you had sexual relations with Dr. Dintleman, we'll start from there."

"You already know that we had sex. My cells would have been on the outside of a condom," Emily replied tartly.

"Yes, but we weren't sure which ones were yours," Sophia couldn't resist pulling her chain. "We, of course, will need fingerprints and a DNA sample from you before you leave."

Emily was fully prepared for that. "Yes, my dad told me to give you those. No need to have the papers reporting you had to get a warrant."

"Did you and Dr. Dintleman have sex on a regular basis?"

"Oh, yes. It was usually on Sunday evening. He said he liked to start off the work week relaxed."

"Who else knew about your Sunday evening meetings?"

"Just some friends," Emily was evasive.

"Which friends? I need names."

Emily hesitated then gave the names of some of her sorority sisters; Sophia wrote them down for verification.

"Anyone else?"

Again Emily hesitated, "No. No I don't think so," she spoke while looking up toward the plaques of credentials on the wall behind Sophia's desk.

Sophia interpreted this as a tell; the girl appeared to be withholding information. Time to try another tack. "Do you remember what time you left Dr. Dintleman's?"

"Yes (this answer was easier). I left at 6:30. I checked my clock when I turned out onto Highway 22, and it was 6:35. I was right on time."

"Right on time for what?"

Emily looked down toward her lap this time. She had clearly given out more information than planned. "I was expected back at the sorority by 7:00."

"What were you expected back for?"

"I was meeting someone." Then she quickly added, "someone to tutor."

"Do you tutor often?"

"Oh, yes, every Sunday night," Emily tried to make herself look as if she were a concerned academic. "I've been tutoring guys from the football team."

The football team? Give me a break. There's more to this than she's letting on. Sophia continued her line of questioning. "That's an admirable activity. Who were you tutoring Sunday night, and in what subject?"

"Well, I usually tutor J'Dane Warford, one of the line-backers. I've been helping him with his writing."

"Spell that, would you," Sophia was ready to probe in another area. "Now, how long does it take for you to get from Dr. Dintleman's back to campus? Did you notice what time you got back?"

"Um, about 20 minutes if I hit all the lights. I didn't check my phone, but I had time to change before J'Dane came by."

Sophia wanted to ask Emily why she needed to change clothes to tutor J'Dane, but she decided to let it alone for now. She thanked her and gave her a card with office numbers then let her leave. As soon as Emily was out of sight, Sophia was on the horn to her investigative assistant, Donny. "I need you to act fast before too many people get their stories straight. Find out what you can about an MNSU football player, J'Dane (she spelled it) Warford. He's supposed to be getting tutoring from Emily Leonard on Sunday nights. And find out what her Sunday night schedule has been looking like. She seems to be awfully busy on Sundays. Oh, and by the way, get us a picture of this football guy."

22

Like many Dardanelle men, Donny was on a first name basis with the MNSU football coach. Donny had provided security for big games from time-to-time and was comfortable asking questions about one of the players (just to check someone else's alibi). What he learned was suggestive, but not definite.

It seemed that J'Dane was very popular with the sorority girls on campus and had dated several of them. His current love interest was very high maintenance. Her father was some fancy lawyer up at Springdale. He had met her through a tutoring program at the Student Learning Center last semester. Coach had the idea that the relationship had advanced beyond platonic, but he held his tongue when J'Dane got dressed up every Sunday evening ostensibly to go to his tutoring session.

When Donny went by the sorority house (just to check someone else's alibi), Emily was not around, but a chatty young thing with lots of kohl on her eyes and a very short skirt was just full of information. Yes, there had been a tutoring program last fall, but not now. Some of the sisters still hang out with some of the guys, but there isn't much tutoring going on. Mostly it's just hanging out, watching games on TV and studying together. Except for Emily Leonard and J'Dane Warford. They clearly have a thing for each other. Every Sunday night, Emily rushes home from her sessions with Dr. Dintleman just in time to change clothes and go out with J'Dane. Everybody loves J'Dane. He's so nice and so smart, and he's a premed major.

Of course everyone was shocked when they heard about Dr. Dintleman the next day. Emily had locked herself in her room for hours. Poor girl; now she'd have to find someone else to help her work through her anger issues with her father. He's a big shot in Springdale, and he wants her to be a lawyer. And, he doesn't want her to date J'Dane because he's black.

—◊◊◊—

When Donny returned early that afternoon with his information and the picture of J'Dane, Sophia was at the big white board working on a timeline. "Let's see now," she used what the students and Dewey had told her. "He was alive when Emily Leonard left at 6:30, according to her. And he was dead when Melissa Owens arrived at 7:05, according to her. Dewey estimates he saw the big SUV at about 7:00. That gives our killer a 30 minute window. Emily says she didn't pass any vehicles, so the killer must have either already been on Bobcat Hollow, or entered after 6:35 when she checked her watch.

"Because of the force of the bludgeoning," she continued, "we think the killer was a man. Who are our likely suspects? Dewey Elkins was in town about 6:30. He claims he got back to the bridge a little before 7:00. If he pushed it, he might have had time to kill Michael. He could have pulled that bicycle off the road so nobody would see him. But we don't have any motive.

"We have the assumed killer who drives a big SUV. And we have D'Jane Warford. From the looks of him, he's plenty big enough to do the job. Could have followed Emily out there. Maybe a fit of jealousy?"

"Yeah," Donny suggested, "but if he was there for Dewey to see just before 7:00, then how did he get back to campus (and probably change clothes) in time to meet Emily? And, does he drive a big SUV? That kind of vehicle seems too 'old man' for a college boy. And, what about Emily's father? Evidently he disapproves of her dating a black man."

"What about the husband of that crazy girl who lived with Dintleman before she ran off to Atlanta? Didn't he threaten to kill the doctor?" Donny offered.

"Yes, but we don't even know where he is. If he's in Atlanta, he's a little far for a Sunday evening hit job. Damn," Sophia was perplexed. "we don't have much of a case, do we? Well, let's nail down where all these folks were. If we can shave a little off this timeline, we can start looking for discrepancies. Meanwhile, we have lots of people to interview. What with his practice and his research, our Dr. Dintleman must have had some skeletons. We need to find out which one killed him."

23

When Garnet's past student, the sex offender, Seth Gunter, had "slithered" away from local law enforcement, he headed straight for a known port of refuge in Conway, Delilah Davenport. Delilah was a porn queen of sorts who ran her own business. She had a ready stable of young lovelies from the University of Central Arkansas eager to pick up some extra cash. Delilah was an expert in makeup and hair. When she finished with colored contacts, expensive wigs and professional makeup, no one would recognize her girls. Tattoos had become a bit of a problem, but she had experimented with plaster mixes until she could cover almost anything.

Her on-line business was special in that it featured mostly girl-girl videos and close-up pics. Occasionally when someone like Seth was around, she'd do a heterosexual shoot, paying him quite well by the hour. Sometimes the great Delilah herself would star in a film just to pander to her fan base. Her studio was well-equipped with cameras and lights, and for those reluctant performers, she had hidden cameras for a soft, muted background that usually enhanced the "romantic" look of her highly scripted scenarios.

Seth loved the big comfy bed with the hidden cameras. He had shot several videos of himself with unsuspecting lovelies. His deal with Delilah was that he promoted his own work and paid her for studio time. He had been able so far to support himself in good, middle-class style. What he hadn't told Delilah was that he had shot several videos and pics of under-age children (he knew her well enough to know she'd kick his hiney straight to Hell if she ever found out). He figured what she didn't know wouldn't hurt her. Seth enjoyed the adult porn, and he could get his rocks off looking at it. But what really thrilled him was the child pornography. Some nights he couldn't wait to close his bedroom door and look at his increasingly large collection.

He never stayed at Delilah's more that a couple of days. It was too risky for both of them. Delilah would advance him enough cash to rent a mid-priced apartment, and he would work it off in her studio. She had an old beat up Nissan that she kept licensed. He'd park his current vehicle (a Lincoln Navigator) inside her garage, and no one would be the wiser. All-in-all, it was a win-win situation.

Delilah wasn't the only one who sheltered Seth. Since he had branched out into child pornography, he had met some cool dudes. He had an agreement with the owner of Tony's Pizza Parlor. Seth could sell his adult porn packaged and hidden in the box under a pizza order. And he could slip in an occasional child pic for his special customers as long as the owner got first dibs on his new stuff. It wasn't long before Seth was once again financially solvent.

The viewers and purveyors of child porn were not a particularly wealthy group. In fact child porn didn't demand very high prices. It was the anticipation of the titillating rush that drove the practice forward. The group of psychologically obsessive men (and a few women) fed each other's insatiable need for the perverted images of children being sexually abused.

24

After the shock of learning who her father was, Bennie Sue was relieved when Della said she was too busy to see her that night for a face-to-face. Della was working days now at the Johnson County Hospital. Her next day off would be Thursday. She agreed to be home in the afternoon for whatever "really important" talk Bennie Sue wanted to have. Della didn't even bother to ask.

An apprehensive Bennie Sue took the afternoon off from work and headed out to Lamar Thursday at noon. The relationship with her mother had become almost nonexistent. The only thing that still held them together was Bennie's concern for her sister. Cheyenne was 17 now, a junior in high school. Bennie still called her several times a month, but found keeping contact progressively more difficult. Cheyenne was her mother's daughter. Boys and parties took up almost all of her attention. It didn't pay to call her on weekends when they might have had an honest conversation while Della was at work because, more often than not, Cheyenne was sleeping off last night's party or busy getting ready for tonight's.

Bennie Sue took the Lamar exit off I-40 then turned right onto Horse Head Road. Della's mobile home was about a mile down the road under the one scraggly tree on her lot. Additional trailers were on scattered lots nearby. When Cheyenne started school, Della often worked extra hours. She had saved enough to move out here during Bennie's senior year at Pottsville. Living out here left her some privacy and gave her a short drive into Clarksville to the hospital. She would have made better pay with a BSN, but all her college classes were too old, and she would have had to repeat all of them. Bumping up to RN from an LPN had been a much better solution.

Della's double-wide had the faded, aged look that matched the others nearby. The driveway was washed out rock, and a few neglected flowers sat in pots beside the wooden steps at the front door. Bennie Sue took a deep breath and pushed the tiny circle for the door bell.

Della opened the door and turned on her heel moving toward the patio door out the back, not saying a word. Bennie Sue followed her dutifully to the covered deck where two wind chimes sang intermittently. Della plopped her butt down onto a padded glider and reached for the rocks glass on the table beside her. "There's stuff in the fridge if you want something," she offered.

The "stuff in the fridge" was mostly beer and tonic water. Della didn't drink beer, so it had to be for someone else, maybe even Cheyenne. Bennie Sue fixed herself a drink in the one clean glass left in the cabinet. She mixed some tonic water with a little margarita mix and some ice then went back outside.

"I needed to ask you about my father," Bennie Sue started tentatively as Della sipped her drink and gazed past her.

"That son of a bitch is still in prison, and he can rot there!" Della's tone was caustically dismissive. "What do you want to know about him? I think you knew him better than I did." She had never gotten over the habit of trying to control her daughter with shame.

"Not him," Bennie Sue spoke slowly and clearly. "My real father."

"Say what?" Della was actually looking straight at Bennie Sue now.

"My real father. James Blackwell is not my father. I have the DNA evidence to prove it."

Della tried one more feint, "Of course he's your father. His name is on your birth certificate. There's some kind of mix up with your DNA, or whatever. That lab of yours isn't perfect, you know."

"I know," Bennie Sue ignored the jab. "That's why we tested it twice. James Blackwell's DNA wasn't in our base. He was processed before we began collecting data. So we had the prison send us a copy of their files. It isn't anywhere close."

Della's expression became closed and almost sly as she processed Bennie Sue's information. "Then you must know who it is, or you wouldn't be here, now would you?"

"You know I can't talk about any of our data, not even to you," Bennie tried to make Della feel more important. Sometimes that ploy worked. "You're the only one I can turn to. I really need to know. It's driving me crazy."

Della sat silently, staring at the floor. Then her face relaxed, almost with relief. "Well, if you know who it is, you know more than me." She shook her head slowly, trying to process the information. Then she laughed. "Well I'll be. After all these years. Lordy, Lordy, it's hard to believe."

Della fell silent, staring vacantly out across the yard. "Mom," Bennie Sue asked quietly, although she didn't feel quiet inside, "Mom, are you going to tell me?"

Della waved a hand at her, brushing her off as if she were a gnat. "Yeah, yeah, I'll tell you. Let me get another drink, and I'll tell you," she seemed resigned to the inevitable. She fixed herself a double in the kitchen then returned to the glider, pulling her legs up under her and getting comfortable.

"By the time I got out of high school I was wild. Believe you me, I had done it all. But for some reason I didn't like the dope. I loved the drinking," she held up her glass for emphasis, "and the screwing. I couldn't get enough of either. Sometimes I'd wake up wondering where I was, but I always had a good looking guy in the sack with me. It's curious to think about now, but even with my 'high risk' behavior, I was actually pretty careful. I got my mini-pills from the Health Department, and always, well almost always, insisted on condoms. I liked it bare-back too, just like everyone else, but no way was I getting herpes or warts, or whatever." She paused to take a long swig of her drink, then fell silent, remembering.

"My freshman year at college was probably the best time I ever had. I hated the dorm, but all the freshmen had to stay in the dorms or at home, and no way was I staying at home! Anyway," she continued, "me and this other girl on my floor, Barbara (we all called her Barbie), hit it off really well. We thought we were really hot stuff. And I guess we were.

"Anyway, we were going through the men on campus like we were in a candy store. The flavor didn't matter. Chocolate, spice, whatever. Umm, umm, that was good stuff! Then we sorta settled on fraternities. Our favorite was Tau, Tau, Tau, the triple Taus. Those boys knew how to party! They didn't have keggers; they had 'bottled water' parties. They filled up those big ole heavy bottles you see on water dispensers with the most wonderful stuff you could imagine. My favorite was the fuzzy navel made with fresh peaches and vodka.

"Me and Barbie had us one hell of a time that fall semester. I think we both slept with every Tau in the house. They were nice about cleanin' up their rooms before parties so the beds didn't stink and there wasn't any hair in the sinks.

"I kept my grades up just enough to get by, and I had to promise Momma I'd do better in the spring so she'd let me go back. I hated going home over Christmas break. But I guess it was just as well. There weren't any parties since all the guys were gone, and I really didn't want to mess around with anyone I went to high school with.

"I was out at Buster's one night with a girl friend who was home from UofA, and this real good lookin' guy asked me to dance. He actually knew how to dance! Not like most of the goof-balls around here. It was James, of course. He was a little older with an engineering degree and lots of money to spend, just on little ole me, and man could he fuck!

"We were goin' to go over to Oklahoma City to party, but I got sick. I was so stopped-up I couldn't hardly breathe, and then it went to bronchitis. I coughed up yellow gup until Momma made me go get some antibiotics just before I started back to school. I was feelin' pretty good, but was on a second round of antibiotics when school started. James had to go to Atlanta to check on some communication towers, so of course I got lonely. Barbie talked me into goin' to a water party with her at the Taus, and I must admit that I had a wonderful time.

"By the end of January when I hadn't had my period, I started countin' back. I had heard that you could get pregnant on the mini-pill if you took antibiotics. I had taken two rounds. And I had to admit to some 'unprotected' sex with James (and a couple of the Taus). Yep. I was pregnant!"

Della closed her eyes and smiled softly, shaking her head as if to say, "I still don't believe it." Then she continued with a sadness to her face, "There went everything. All my dreams. All my plans. I was goin' to get my BSN so I could travel around with James when he had to go out of state for three or four months. I was so sick I couldn't even go to my classes, let alone party. I guess you were lucky. Every time I drank, I puked. No fetal alcohol syndrome for you, Kiddo.

"So, I married James. He was real excited about the baby; he wanted a girl. He made plenty of money, so money wasn't a problem. But I knew I was a failure. Every time I looked at a boy from the time I was 12 years old, my momma called me a whore and told me I'd end up pregnant and fat, raising a bunch of kids by myself just like she did. I didn't want you. But I didn't have the guts to get rid of you. All I could think was that it served me right!

"I dropped out of school until you were born in October. I stayed home with you a couple of months then went down to Morrilton to get my RN degree. I'd planned to finish a BSN on-line later, but that never happened."

"What did you do with me while you went to school?" Bennie Sue wondered.

"Oh, that was easy," Della said disgustedly. "My momma couldn't wait to get her hands on you. She didn't have any use for me, but she sure loved you.

And," she paused for effect, "James couldn't get enough of you. If Momma couldn't keep you, why, he'd just take you with him, as long as it wasn't to work. He was some kind of proud of you!

"I didn't think much of it when I started workin' nights. He didn't seem to mind keepin' you and puttin' you to bed. And it was a way for me to get some fresh air. It was like if I was workin' maybe I wasn't such a big failure after all. We didn't have much of a sex life, workin' different shifts and all. I guess he was too busy lookin' at porn and jacking off to care. But I SWEAR to you, I didn't know what he was doin' to you."

Della turned a pitiful face to Bennie Sue, with tears sliding down her cheeks. "I loved him. I didn't at first, but it didn't take long. I could'a forgiven him for what he did to you if he'd promised me he wouldn't do it no more. And I always thought he was your daddy and he deserved another chance. But I had to divorce him. Thirty years was just too long. Now you're tellin' me even that was a lie."

Della drained her drink, squared her shoulders, and stood up a little unsteadily. "You better go on home," she told Bennie Sue. "I got me some drinkin' and some thinkin' to do. I'll talk to you later." She headed to the kitchen to fix another drink.

Bennie Sue held her tongue and let herself out the front door. Della still hadn't told her who her father was. There was a good chance that Della didn't know.

25

Bennie Sue didn't sleep well Thursday night and showed up to work Friday with shadows under her eyes. She kept checking the clock and called her Aunt Alexis at school during the lunch break. "Mom screwed me again!" Bennie Sue burst out.

"Is it something we can talk about now? Or can it wait 'til dinner?" Alexis guessed that a counseling section was coming up.

"It's not something I want to discuss on the phone. Can I come over tonight? I'll bring a pizza. Will Cynthia be there?"

"No, Cynthia is going to a big party, and she'll spend the night at the sorority house. It's actually about the best time you could come. And I want mushrooms on my pizza."

Bennie Sue hung up then sat back in her chair to do some deep breathing. She was really getting freaked out about this paternity thing.

Bennie Sue ordered a pizza from Simple Simons and stopped to pick it up on her way out of town. Alexis was still in the smallish house that her ex had left her in the divorce settlement, the house where Bennie Sue had found refuge during her high school years. Aunt Alexis had replaced the siding and painted the trim last year, and a new flower bed along the front was waiting for seasonal flowers. A Pottsville Apache wreath incorporating a ball and bat still festooned the front door where Bennie Sue knocked and entered. Her cousin, Cynthia, at 18 was now a talented pitcher for UCA.

As Bennie Sue carried the pizza down the short hall between the kitchen and dining room, she smiled when she saw the pictures of herself in her softball uniform, exactly where they had been for almost eight years. There had been lots of pictures and holiday meals since then, but that time represented the difficult passage Bennie Sue and Alexis had made together.

Alexis had made a small salad, and the two women feasted on the pizza and drank colas. Alexis didn't do alcohol. Something about her dad. After she heard what Bennie Sue's new discovery was and how Della had reacted to the news, Alexis looked down at her lap for a few seconds then began talking in a soft voice.

"Your momma and I were polar opposites. We slept in the same double bed from the time we were little kids all through high school, but that was about the only thing we shared. That and our dad. Daddy was mean as a feral hog, and when he got liquored up, you'd better watch out. I know Momma was afraid of him. If something went wrong, he used her for his punching bag. We had two brothers, as you know, and they could do anything they wanted to. But not us girls. We had to toe the line when Daddy was around.

"When Della was about eight, I guess, Daddy started coming to get her at night. She never would say anything, and I was a little jealous that he liked her better than me. So one night I piped up and teased her, 'Daddy's little pet; Daddy's little pet. What's so special about you anyway?' Daddy looked at me and hooked his finger. 'You want to come?' he asked. 'Well, come on.'

"I was already 11 by then. I'd got my period, and my breasts were big enough for a training bra. I was really proud that I was growing up. I'd seen plenty of pictures of glamorous women with beautiful hair and lots of cleavage at the grocery store check-out. I couldn't wait! I couldn't believe what he did to me," she lowered her voice. "He threw me on my back and yanked my panties off. Then he stuck his hand between my legs and pushed two fingers up my vagina. The pain was awful. It felt like he'd stuck a knife up me. Of course I started to scream, but he clamped his hand over my mouth, and I'll never forget what he said, 'If you ever say a word about this to anyone, I swear I'll cut off those little tits you're so proud of. Now spread your legs out.'"

"He didn't, did he?" Bennie Sue was incredulous.

"Yes, he did, but it was just that one time. I don't know how Della stood it. She was younger than me. No hormones yet. She probably has scars inside of her."

"When did it stop?" Bennie Sue was horrified.

"Not for a while. I was so scared, I went around with my arms crossed over my chest. Momma would ask me what was wrong, but there was no way I was going to tell. It was probably two months after that, Della had been vomiting with a stomach ache when he came for her. I remember her kind of whining and trying to get out of it. But he waived his index finger in her face, and she shut up pronto.

After that I was afraid he was going to kill us. So I told Momma, although I suspect she already knew. She was really upset. Maybe she'd been thinking it really wasn't all that bad. I know now denial is a big part of the pathology. She promised she'd get us away from him, but she didn't say how or when. She said later that he'd told her he'd hunt her down and kill her if she ever tried to leave him."

"So what happened?" Bennie Sue was glued to her seat.

"The accident," Alexis stated flatly. "He was down in Russellville drinking, and no one knows why, but he decided to walk across the railroad tracks there on Commerce."

"Didn't a train hit him?"

"No, it wasn't quite that simple. A train was coming, and the lights were on, and the gates were down. Evidently, he was just standing there on the sidewalk waiting. Then this idiot decides to drive around the gates at 40 mph, and he hit Daddy and threw him so that he landed on the concrete there on the back of his neck. Poof. Just like that," she spread her hands in a 'magic' gesture.

Alexis got up from the small kitchen table and started a pot of coffee. Who cared if they stayed up all night? It was time some skeletons were cleared out of the family closet.

"I remember when they came to tell us." she continued. "I was scared when the Sheriff's Deputy came to our door. I thought maybe they were coming to get Daddy for some fool thing he'd done while he was drunk. When Momma heard the news she sat down in the big rocker and covered her face. She sat there rocking for the longest time while Della and I just sat on the couch. Then she said, 'You girls go on to bed now. I've got some things to take care of in town.' And she went out and got in the Sheriff's car and disappeared. That night Della and I held hands in bed. It wasn't a strong bond, but it was the only one we'd had for a long time."

"Was that the end of it?" Bennie Sue had to ask.

"No, Honey. You know it wasn't the end of it. I don't think there'll ever be an end to it."

"No I guess not," Bennie Sue agreed based on her own experience.

"How about some pie with that coffee? Then I'll tell you what I know about your 'father'." Alexis stood up, trying to break the tension she had created.

"Sure" Bennie agreed. She was certainly in the mood for some comfort food just about now.

"Della and I were already different, but Daddy's death seemed to send us off in different ways. I loved school and reading. I was an honor roll student, and I did lots of things, even softball," she recalled. "But not your momma! She couldn't sit still long enough to finish anything. She probably had ADHD, but she was never diagnosed. I always figured she'd just got one of Daddy's drunken sperm. If there was anyone who had rum balls, it was Daddy."

The two women started in on their pie, and Alexis continued. "I hate to say it, but Della was the stereotypical 'easy girl' in high school. I swear she screwed everything in pants in the whole county!" Bennie Sue couldn't help but think of Cheyenne. "And it didn't get any better when she went to MNSU," Alexis shook her head, remembering. "I think she went to every frat party on campus her first semester. They talk about guys having contests to see how many women they can hook up with. Della had them beat. It was like she had a weekly quota to meet.

"From what she said, she really had the hots for Michael Dintleman. She was over at the Tau Tau Tau house all the time. He is the one isn't he?" Bennie Sue nodded, knowing she was not authorized to release the information yet. "But that cooled some when she met James. I think she really was in love with him. She just didn't seem to know how to corral herself. It was like something was missing, and she just kept running, chasing after something out there that would make her happy."

26

Alexis tried to get Bennie Sue to spend the night. Bennie Sue demurred. She knew Aunt Alexis was trying to comfort her, but she preferred to be alone. What Bennie Sue didn't know was that it was Aunt Alexis who needed comfort, and who was hoping that she could keep her mind off the past if Bennie Sue were there.

Alexis had been over the Daddy story hundreds of times, and the emotional impact was further and further away as time passed, especially since the immediate family had been pretty open about the problem once Daddy passed. Her mother was determined that Daddy's relatives were not going to turn the SOB into a saint!

The thing that Alexis hadn't been open with was her ex, Grant Cavenaugh. The pair had divorced very suddenly when their daughter Cynthia was five and Bennie Sue was eleven. Everyone assumed that Grant must have been cheating on her. If they only knew!

Things were going well that spring. Cynthia at five was a pure delight. She loved to dress up in long dresses and fix her own hair. Alexis smiled as she remembered Cynthia coming our of her room with every hairclip she owned fastened in her hair. Bennie Sue was doing well too. She had started making friends as soon as she started in her new school, and she was signed up for 12-and-under softball this summer. It was a big change for her.

Bennie Sue's social life wasn't the only change. She was full-throttle into puberty. She had recognizable breasts and the beginnings of axillary and pubic hair. Deodorant was a must now, and her menstrual cycle couldn't be far off. Alexis noticed some of the neighborhood boys starting to come around. And she noticed that Bennie Sue was oblivious to the sexual innuendos some of the boys offered.

"Bennie Sue, what was Joel doing just now with his hands all over you?" Alexis remembered asking.

"Oh, he was just checking to see if I have a perfect figure," Bennie Sue had responded innocently.

"Bennie Sue! What he's doing is called getting fresh. All he's trying to do is get to feel you without getting his face slapped. Next thing you know he'll move from looking up the legs of your shorts every time you spread your legs out to trying to get a feel there too! That's what boys do when they want to have sex with you."

Bennie Sue just stood there; it was just beginning to dawn on her what had been going on. Meanwhile Cynthia piped up, "Yeah, just the way my daddy does to me."

Just the way my daddy does to me. Alexis froze in place, trying to hide her reaction and give herself time to think. Those few words had just turned her whole world upside down. She pretended nothing had happened and sent the girls on a bike ride down to the park with Cynthia trailing behind Bennie Sue on her little pink bike with sparkly streamers and training wheels.

When the girls came back Alexis took the bull by the horns and coaxed her daughter to tell her what she and Daddy did that was "just like" what Alexis had been warning Bennie Sue about. Cynthia was very forthcoming in her innocence. Daddy liked to rub her titties and between her legs where it felt good. She in turn would rub his boy thing to make it get big. Alexis remembered when Cynthia was two years old. She liked to go into the bathroom with her daddy. Alexis could still remember Cynthia coming out of the bathroom in her little yellow jumper, her shrill little voice piping, "Penis, I like him;" or, "Penis, I don't like him."

Later that night when Bennie Sue asked about it, Alexis lied and told her Cynthia thought snuggling and wrestling with her daddy were the same thing the boys were doing with Bennie Sue.

It was not the same thing! How could she have been so blind? She had thought that Grant accepted Bennie Sue's dilemma. He had been very supportive of the whole idea of adding Bennie Sue to their little family. Had he intended to prey on the young girl? Alexis was sure Bennie Sue would have given her some hint if Grant had been molesting her. But why had he passed her by? Then Alexis remembered. Her dad had bypassed her for her younger sister. Dad and Grant both liked them young!

Alexis was nearly overcome with the reverberating guilt. *How could I have missed it? I should have caught it. Don't women know what their husbands do? I'm an elementary teacher, for God's sake. I've seen the signs in other little girls. How could I have missed it in my own daughter?*

Then there was the fact of her own come-down. In her mind, she could imagine Della's accusations, *"You thought you were so smart, didn't you? Little miss perfect school teacher! You thought you were better than me. But you weren't. You never were better than me!"*

She's right, Alexis ranted at herself. *I was getting my degree while Della was running around screwing everything in pants. Then she married someone who abused her child. I felt so superior. I was wrong. I was wrong. I was wrong. I married someone who was just like James Blackwell! How could we both have made the same mistake? Wasn't Daddy enough? Is it genetic?*

———✦———

Grant had left the house that night, but he didn't go willingly nor quietly. He never denied that he had been sexually abusing his own daughter. "What's the big deal?" he had whined. "It doesn't hurt them.

Look at Bennie Sue. She's fine, probably hoping some guy will knock her up."

"What is the matter with you?" Alexis had countered. "Do you not remember that James Blackwell was sentenced to 30 years in prison? And that he will be required to register as a sex offender? And do you not see that that's what you are--A SEX OFFENDER?"

Grant had offered several self-serving arguments, hoping to mollify Alexis. She wasn't buying it. "You get your things, and you get out now, tonight. You can come back this weekend to get the rest of your stuff, but you will never live in this house again. And you had better get yourself a lawyer because I certainly am." Alexis had the locks changed the next day.

27

On Monday, Bennie Sue stuck her head inside Dr. Garnet Daniels's office to ask Garnet when she had time for a little chat. Bennie Sue had had quite a few chats with Garnet when she was a student at MNSU. Garnet was the type of professor who would give you straight, no-bull advice and wouldn't spread your business all over campus. Garnet was heading out to classes, but she agreed to meet Bennie Sue at 4:00 that afternoon.

Dr. Daniels was a reproductive anatomist of some renown. Her research on vaginal anatomy made her the butt of quite a few jokes, but it also provided lots of consulting opportunities and the occasional expert witness testimony in court cases. It was Dr. Daniels who had encouraged Bennie Sue to pursue her forensic certification and recommended her for her current job.

"I guess you've heard about my genetic situation?" A very tense Bennie Sue started off after she was seated in a comfortable chair next to Garnet's desk.

Garnet shook her head. "No. I don't think so."

"Oh, well," Bennie Sue was pleased that her colleagues at the lab had held her information confidential, as it was intended to be, "it seems that James Blackwell is not really my father after all. We got a match on the blood samples that came in after the murder. Michael Dintleman was my father!"

Garnet's look was incredulous. She got up from her desk immediately and shut the office door. "Oh my, that's a bit of a shock, isn't it?"

"I didn't believe it at first." Bennie Sue continued. "But Steve Hoyle ran it several times. And the system always shows a match. I really don't know how to react. I was going to him for counseling, and now he's dead. And he was my FATHER."

The look of anguish on Bennie Sue's face pulled at Garnet's maternal instinct. She wanted to say, "There, there," and pat her on the back, but that wasn't what she thought Bennie Sue needed. Instead, she reached to the edge of the desk and covered Bennie Sue's hand with her own. "Let's see what we can do," she offered. "Are you sleeping?" Bennie Sue shook her head. "Are you eating?" Bennie Sue nodded and nodded, indicating she was eating too much.

"OK, let's get you some relief. Would you be willing to see Dr. Frank Norton? He's my doctor. He's pretty laid back and non-threatening. I think he can help you, at least for the short term."

As Bennie Sue seemed to relax a little, Garnet continued, "What do you make of your genetic conundrum? Are you an only child, or do you have a slew of siblings and cousins running around out there?"

"I don't know!" Bennie Sue was emphatic. "And I'm really not sure how to go about finding out. I Googled 'Michael Dintleman' and got a lot of his professional stuff, but I don't really know where to start on the relatives thing."

"I can help you with that. Or to be more precise, I know someone who can help you with that. One of my good friends is Carolyn Melissa McAlister who recently retired from MNSU. Carolyn Melissa just happens to be a genealogy genius. She knows how to search every data base you can think of. If Michael Dintleman has relatives out there, she can find them. And, I just thought of this, you may be in line for some inheritance. You never can tell."

"That's a scary thought."

Garnet nodded in agreement. "Tell you what, let me call Dr. Norton and Carolyn Melissa to set things up for you. Then you can contact them yourself and go from there."

Bennie Sue smiled and nodded her acceptance. Then her face became sober again. "There's one more thing I need to talk to you about," she looked at the clock, "if you have time."

"Sure," Garnet agreed, thinking to herself, *She's pregnant.*

"I talked to Aunt Alexis last weekend, and she told me my Grandpa Webb raped both her and my mother when they were little girls. The way she told it, she would have been about 11, and it was probably only once, but he did it to my mother all the time, and she was only nine when he got killed in an accident. I know that my mother had a C-section with both me and my little sister, so I was just wondering...," she trailed off.

"Would she have had internal scars that made a vaginal delivery risky?" Garnet finished the thought.

Bennie Sue nodded agreement, and Garnet got up to search her file cabinet.

"Here it is," she pulled out an orange file folder. "At birth, the vagina is only about one-½ inch long with a hymen of about one-fourth inch.. Growth in length and elasticity is very slow until female hormones are secreted. Vaginal length in childhood increases as the girl grows, up to two-¼ inch with a hymen of about one-half inch, about the size of your little finger. Considering that the average penis is one inch in diameter and about six inches long, although the entire length is not inserted during intercourse, penetration of a child by an adult is guaranteed to cause tearing!"

"Oh, my," Bennie Sue was appalled. "No wonder the State of Arkansas considers any penetration in a child under 11 years of age to be considered as rape. But," she continued, "Della was sexually active, evidently very active. Wouldn't she have had painful intercourse?"

"Not necessarily. The age at menarche (beginning of menses) varies considerably. Anything between nine and 16 is 'normal'. Some estrogen can be detected as early as two-½ years before the first period. The vagina lengthens and the introitus (opening) widens so that at menarche, the length can be anywhere from three to four-½ inches long with an opening of about one inch. The change in length and elasticity could have been enough to prevent painful intercourse as an adult. However," she continued, "the situation is different at child-birth where a three-½ to four inch baby's head is forced through the vagina. Here old scars could really increase the danger of excessive tearing."

Garnet made photocopies of her data on vaginal dimensions and told Bennie Sue she'd call after she had talked to Dr. Norton and Carolyn Melissa McAlister. She shook her head slowly after Bennie Sue left. What a mess! The poor girl had a lot to deal with.

28

After her conversation with Garnet about Della's possible injuries, something else popped up that was bound to worry Bennie Sue's mind. Steve Hoyle had made another discovery when he was finishing up the large mass of fingerprints and miscellaneous DNA from the crime site. Just before 5:00, Bennie Sue had been called into Hattie West's office where Detective Sergeant Calypso was seated, waiting.

"OK, Guys, we've got some new information I need to share. Looks like there's another finger in the pot that you both need to know about. It seems that Dewey Elkins is Michael Dintleman's half-brother," she spoke emphatically. "I haven't run down all the loose ends on the genealogy, but the DNA is pretty clear." She sat back in her chair and waited for it to hit the fan.

"You mean I have even more relatives?" Bennie was dumbfounded. "This can't be happening. Who is this Dewey Elkins? Does he live around here?"

"Damn him!" Sophia interjected. "Yes he lives around here. I've known him for years. He's that

Vet with PTSD that lives out there by Dintleman. He has a big ole house about a half mile west, but he doesn't stay in it. He's built himself an elaborate camp down on the creek so he can stay outside. Says he doesn't like to be shut in. I can't believe he didn't tell me. Wait 'til I get my hands on him!"

"Is he a suspect?" Bennie Sue was confused.

"No, not until now," Sophia admitted. "But if he's a half-brother, it's possible he was in line to inherit something. And that gives him motive. Plus, he found what appears to be the murder weapon. And he could have planted it."

The three looked at each other somberly. This could be bad business.

Sophia cautioned Bennie Sue about contacting Dewey. "I don't want him to know about you until his alibi is cleared, so don't make any plans to meet him yet. If he's dirty, you could be in real danger. Understood?"

Bennie Sue had another question. "I know I'm not allowed to work on the case, but can I still look at the genealogy? I just talked to Dr. Daniels, and she is going to put me in contact with someone named Carolyn Melissa McAlister who is supposed to be some type of expert on family trees. There may be others, and it wouldn't hurt to find out now."

—⚊⚊—

Carolyn Melissa McAlister was indeed an expert on genealogical searches. During her last three years at the MNSU library, she had started searching her own roots and had become a resource for area people. Her short booklet, *Finding Yourself Through Them*, was a huge success for lay researchers and had brought her several interesting consulting jobs since her retirement. She started immediately when Garnet called her about Bennie Sue's connection to Dr. Dintleman and already had something to report.

Carolyn Melissa lived in a large log cabin out west of Dardanelle, not too far from Dr. Dintleman's house. She came from Scotch-Irish stock on one side, and English on the other. Her husband, Mark, was from Prussian and English stock. Between them, they had ancestors in both the Revolutionary and the Civil Wars. The inside of the cabin was decorated with antiques from both eras. Stern-faced settlers and handsome soldiers stared down from the walls. Memorabilia from York Town and Gettysburg were proudly displayed along with muskets, iron pots, and a spinning wheel. The cabin was a little museum of American heritage.

In stark contrast to the log cabin, the large addition on the back was strictly modern. Carolyn Melissa's office was filled with sagging bookshelves and tables piled high with books, newspapers, tablets, etc. Bennie Sue didn't know how the genealogist ever found anything. But like many highly cerebral people with obsessive tendencies, Carolyn Melissa knew exactly where everything was.

"Here," she directed Bennie Sue, pulling a heavily marked tablet from under the pile beside her computer, "I thought I'd take a little peek before you got here." Bennie Sue took the chair next to the desk after Carolyn Melissa scooted a big pile of papers onto the floor. "This is really fascinating," she shoved the unintelligible markings toward Bennie Sue. Michael Dintleman was the only child of Horace and Anna Dintleman. Horace and Anna divorced, and both remarried. Horace and his second wife, Deloris, did not have children. But, Anna married Randy Elkins, and they had a son..."

"Dewey!" Bennie Sue jumped in. "We found his DNA match at the lab," she explained.

"Yes, Dewey," Carolyn Melissa continued. That would make him Michael's half brother."

"Were there any others, or any other children?" Bennie wanted to know.

"Not that I have found. You, of course, are not listed as Michael's child, so there may be more. The same for Dewey--no children listed. But Dewey's step father, Randy, had a daughter, Eileen, (no relation to you) who was seven when Dewey was born. She would be his half sister."

"What about grandparents and cousins?" Bennie Sue asked. "There has to be somebody else. This whole thing seems like such a dead end."

"Well, now that you put it that way, I'm sorry, but both sets of immediate grandparents are deceased. Neither the Dintlemans nor the Elkins seemed to be very prolific, at least not that they recognized legally. But I've just started. Give me several weeks (these things take time), and I'll keep looking. You may turn out to be his only heir. Do you know if he had a will?"

29

Sophia was pissed with Dewey Elkins, and she had worked up a good head of steam stomping her way through the weeds to his camp. Why hadn't he told her? Did he think it was cute for her to have to come all the way back out here?

Dewey must have heard her coming. He was unfolding the rocking chair for her as she approached. "Howdy," he nodded his head in recognition. "What brings you out this fine morning?"

"You can stop with the pleasantries." she laid into him. "You know perfectly well why I'm here. For God's sake, why didn't you tell me he was your brother?"

"Half-brother," Dewey corrected her calmly.

"It doesn't matter, and you know it. Any close relative is a suspect in a murder investigation. For all I know, you put that bat out there yourself and made up a story about some big guy in a big SUV!"

"Weeell," he drew it out. "I can see where you're comin' from. But there's no need to get your panties in a twist. I apologize. I thought the fingerprints and the DNA would take care of it. Besides," he looked at her knowingly, "I was hopin' you'd find a reason to come back out. I kinda like your company."

"Like my company?" she sputtered, caught completely off guard. "Do you have any idea what my life is like, working this investigation? There is no way I have time to think, let alone come out here to keep you company!"

He smiled slightly, enjoying her indignation. "That's all right. There'll be time for that later. I guess you're wantin' to know if I have an alibi? Well, I left Simple Simon's right at 6:30 when the commercials from *60 Minutes* came on. It takes me about half an hour to pedal back out here, and it was dark when I got here. I was pullin' off the road when that SUV stopped. There were several other cars runnin' up and down the road, but I didn't pay much attention until the sirens started."

"Dewey, I'm sorry, but don't you see? If you really pushed it, you might have had time to ride on up to Michael's and get back here before his student found him. That makes you a suspect."

Dewey took in a long breath, "Well, not with me stopping' at Hawthorn's!" he was quite indignant.

"Hawthorn's? You never said anything about Hawthorn's!" she laid into him again.

"I didn't?" He tried to remember. "But I thought I told you."

"No, Sir, not a word."

"Oh," he blushed. "I thought I did. Sometimes I forget things when I get stressed. And losing Michael that way was a bit of stress."

Now she felt sorry for him. She knew about his PTSD, and she was surprised she didn't know that he and Michael were half brothers.

"I always stop by if I have time. I dropped off some bread and milk, and I carried in a couple of loads of wood. Don't want her to get cold on these chilly nights. Old folks get cold a lot easier than we do."

Hawthorn was the 90 year old widow of a local war hero. She still lived by herself in the little cracker box house they had built during the 1950s. Dewey considered it a duty to check on her frequently on his trips into town.

"How long were you there?"

"Umm," he thought about it. "I figure not more than 15 minutes. She had a new kitten she wanted me to see. I guess I'll be haulin' cat food for a while."

"Well," she was relieved, "I guess if you left town at 6:30 and stopped at Hawthorn's for 15 minutes, you really didn't have time to ride down to Michael's and get back to your place by 7:00."

"No," he agreed. "I'm in pretty good shape, but even I couldn't make it that fast. Does this mean you can let me go as a suspect?"

"Yeah, I reckon so," she nodded. "But I still need to talk to Hawthorn."

"That's good, cause' I don't want to get crosswise with you. That'd make it real hard for me to ask you out," he was not one to mince words.

She was caught completely off guard a second time. "Where did that come from? A minute ago you were a murder suspect, and now you're asking me out?"

"Yeah, that's about the size of it. I know you're too busy with this investigation to keep runnin' out here, so I thought we could plan to meet, or something," he trailed off.

"I don't..." she paused. She had been about to say, I don't think that's such a good idea. But instead she blurted out, "I don't have to work Sunday."

His smile lit up the whole world, and she felt she had made the right decision, at least for now.

30

A Friday memorial for Dr. Michael Dintleman was organized on campus by the Psychology Department. The small amphitheater in the Liberal Arts building was packed. Bennie Sue slipped into a row toward the back, hoping to get a look at Dewey Elkins. She'd heard different stories about him and was really curious.

Most people described him as somewhat eccentric, whatever that means. He was a product of Dardanelle who had been the wide receiver on a winning Sand Lizards team and was expected to play college football. He disappointed football fans when he stayed home to take care of his mother who had breast cancer. When she died two years later, he had joined the Army and headed for Afghanistan. Here the story became fuzzy.

When he came back, he was a changed man. It was pretty clear that he suffered from PTSD. His anger was almost palpable, and he was involved in several barroom brawls. Then he withdrew from the towns-people. He set up a camp out near Bobcat Hollow and traveled back and forth to town on a bicycle with a cart. People avoided him because of the brawls, and he didn't seem to mind. He wasn't homeless. He had his mother's old house. He wasn't derelict. He quit drinking at the local bars. He was kind to the elderly. He was one of the locals who watched out for Hawthorn. Some said he was a pauper. Some said he was sitting on a fortune, and some said he had killed his half brother to get his estate. Who was this man?

Dr. Russell began the memorial with a recounting of his having met Dr. Dintleman, how they became friends and research partners. The president of student government praised the man for his involvement in student activities. She presented the Department of Psychology with a plaque commemorating his contributions. Several students, mostly females, spoke about how he had mentored them and helped them gain self confidence to begin to plan for life after MNSU.

When Dewey Elkins stood up, the sniveling from the first several rows stopped. All eyes were on him. Instead of his usual fatigues, he wore a navy blue suit with a soft pink shirt and an emerald and pink striped tie. Instead of his usual boots, he wore oxblood loafers and a matching belt. He was clean shaven, and his hair and beard had been trimmed. His was a commanding presence, so much more because it was unexpected.

"Michael was my half brother. We had the same wonderful mother. She would have been saddened by his death as I am. We were over 10 years apart in age, but we spent time together in summers, even after he started here at MNSU. He was an older brother and mentor to me. I missed him when he went away for his doctorate. And I was grateful that he was here when I came back from Afghanistan. He's the last of my family, and my future will be less certain without him."

With that short eulogy, Dewey Elkins suitably memorialized his brother and gained the respect of many people in the room, including Bennie Sue. She was suddenly excited about meeting her new relative.

31

The Little Miss Pea Vine contest in Memphis on Saturday had taken up most of the week for Cassie and Keith. They had to select outfits and props and take photos of Candy in each costume. They had to photo the costumes themselves to put out on their website after the contest. They had to reconfirm hotel reservations for Friday and Saturday night. A three and ½ hour drive the morning of the pageant and another the evening after was out of the question. They had to pack all the makeup and hair supplies that might be needed. Candie needed a trim on her bangs, and she said her Mary Jane shoes that went with her casual outfit were rubbing her toes. Thankfully the expensive, fully sequined shoes for her other outfits were still fitting her.

Cassie had to have a manicure and a pedicure and have her hairline cleaned up. She tried on outfits until she finally decided what to wear during the pageant. She was going for a gorgeous, but not tacky look. She finally picked a pair of light wool dress slacks and a high end blouse. Four inch heels would give her a little more glamour and accent her long legs. She selected coordinating earrings and a chunky necklace to fill out the ensemble, then threw in a silk scarf in case she didn't want to wear the necklace. Selecting jewelry reminded her that she still needed to pack earring and necklace sets for Candie, no rings.

Keith helped with keeping things organized at home. He had developed a long checklist and schedule just for pageants, and he rigidly adhered to his plan. In addition, at the bank he bought several prepaid VISA cards for shopping after the pageant, and he found the box of discarded apple-green envelopes for lock-box keys he had stored in his office. He had found them to be an excellent way to store the discs from his digital camera for safe keeping.

Keith took off work early Friday. Using his check list, he loaded up his black Cadillac Escalade by himself. He had found that when Cassie helped him, things were very hard to find, or completely missing when they got to a pageant. He put Candie's travel box with toys and travel games and a big fluffy pillow in the back seat. They used this box only for travel so that she wouldn't be so bored during the trip.

The pageant was chaotic as usual. The Little Miss contest was scheduled to start at 11:00 am and run for no more than two hours. Then the group would clear out and the Jr. Miss and Miss contests would follow in the afternoon and evening. The dressing area was a large, open room containing small tables with mirrors around the outside wall and rows through the middle. Rolling clothes racks were positioned to serve four to six contestants. As contestants registered, they were assigned a number then allowed to go find their table and bring their costumes in from the parking lot. Men were allowed to assist with moving heavy suitcases and boxes, but absolutely no men were allowed in the dressing room while the girls were changing.

There were too many contestants to suit Keith. After the street clothes section, he wandered outside where most of the guys had gathered to smoke and talk. He looked around, but didn't see his old buddy, Seth Gunter, who had texted him on his burner phone to bring some lock-box key envelopes to the pageant. Keith wasn't worried, he knew Seth well enough to know he'd be there for sure when the swimsuit competition started, as would be several other "talent scouts" looking for young beauties to photograph.

Sure enough, when the swimsuits started coming out, Keith turned around from his second row seat to see several men he recognized sitting in the back rows with their cameras ready. Seth Gunter caught Keith's eye and winked to acknowledge the contact.

The competition had been whittled down to 10 final contestants, and there were several likely winners. Candie had her work cut out for her. But, as usual, the minute she stepped out onto the stage, she became golden. Nobody could beat her poise and smile. Cassie had picked a little pink bikini to which she had added rose appliqués. The little roses were placed to be subtly suggestive of breasts and a darker pubic area. The next best contestant was a dark haired beauty with enormous soft brown eyes. Her costume was one piece with lots of sequins. Here again, the swirl of sequins created a suggestion of breasts, and a slightly darker crotch.

Keith held his breath as the runners-up were announced. The judges had Candie and the dark eyed beauty step forward. One of these two little girls would become Miss Pea Vine. The auditorium became quiet, waiting for the announcement. The first runner up was the dark haired girl. Candie had won again!

In the hub-bub of little girls crying because they had not been chosen, mothers stridently criticizing the judges, and happy chatter from nearby relatives, Keith had not noticed that Seth had moved just behind him.

"I'll meet you in the parking lot in five minutes," Seth spoke loudly enough for Keith to hear.

The two men met and shook hands in the parking lot then ambled over to the Escalade where Keith had left the box of lock-box envelopes.

"Nice wheels," Seth commented.

"Got to look like a banker," Keith explained. "What are you driving now?

"I got one of those Lincoln Navigators. Black and shiny. Hauls a lot of cargo."

"Where are you living now, you rascal," Keith queried. I thought you were in Clarksville, but someone said you'd moved."

"Yeah, I can't do that sex offender shit! They hauled me in down in Malverne for sex with an underage girl. Hell, she told me she was 16. Her mother turned me in for rape. She knew all the time we were doing it. She just got mad because I was doing her daughter more than I was doing her. Besides the girl really was 16 when the whole thing blew up. They pled me down to indecency with a child, and I'm supposed to register as a sex offender. They'll have to catch me first!"

—⁂—

Candie fell asleep in the back of the Escalade before they crossed the Mississippi bridge, leaving Keith and Cassie to rehash the pageant and to start planning for the Easter Bunny pageant next month. Keith complimented Cassie on her bikini decoration and suggested baby blue might be just the color for Nashville.

"What were all those men in the back doing there?" Cassie asked innocently. "I guess I just never paid attention before, but there seemed to be a lot of them who weren't fathers."

Keith checked the rear-view mirror to be sure Candie really was asleep before answering. "That's one of the unfortunate aspects of beauty pageants for little girls," he explained. "Those men, my dear, are pedophiles."

They stopped at Chuckie Cheese in Conway as a reward for Candie. But the little girl was experiencing after-pageant let down, and was not her usual enthusiastic self. She didn't even want to play "Whack a Mole" with Keith. Sunday was a deliberate "off" day. Keith took Candie to see a Lego movie while Cassie cleaned her costumes so Keith could do photos after work Monday.

Monday, Keith surprised both of them. He brought two beautiful long-stemmed pink silk roses. "One for my Little Miss," he bowed to Candie and presented her with a rose. "And one for my Big Miss," he bowed to Cassie. Then father and daughter moved down the hall to make photographs of her costumes to add to their internet collection.

32

Dewey had called Sophia Friday after the memorial service to confirm their Sunday date. "Do you like to fish?" When she said she did, he continued, "Wear hiking clothes and boots. We may hit some rough stuff. I'll pick you up about 12:30 so you can sleep in (clearly, he knew where she lived and that she needed rest). I'll fix us some lunch when we get there."

Sophia wondered where "there' was going to be, and she wondered how he was going to pick her up on his bicycle. This could be interesting.

Sunday, at 12:30 sharp, Dewey knocked on her door. He led her into the parking lot to a late model Jeep Cherokee. So much for the bicycle. He was quiet as they drove west past Bobcat Hollow to a small road marked Elkins for 911 emergencies. The gravel had recently been graded, so the ride back about three-quarters of a mile was relatively smooth. They pulled up in front of a Victorian style house neatly bordered with white fences and flower beds. Sophia had no idea this house was even here.

She had never had reason to be back this far in her duties.

"I been workin' on these beds," he said dryly. "The daffodils are already gone, but there's hyacinth, and the tulips are comin' up." She could also see various fruit trees and redbuds in bloom. The hollies by the front steps were trimmed, and, overall, the landscaping was very pleasing.

Dewey walked across the deep porch and opened the door for her. The inside was a grand surprise. The wooden floor was polished to a high sheen, with eight inch wallboards, and a soft flowered wall paper that appeared to be new covered the walls up to the high ceiling. The ceiling itself was off-white paneling. The crystal three-tiered chandelier in the center was surrounded by an octagon made up of eight three foot long panels, each covered with coordinated mosaics of softly colored flowers.

"Oh, wow!" Sophia whispered as she stood near the room's center and pivoted around to see each side.

"Like it?" it was a rhetorical question.

"This is marvelous! Where did you find all this?" she waved her arm in a circle.

"It was my mother's. She always wanted a Victorian house. So Daddy built her one when they moved here just after I was born. I was raised here. It went down a lot after Daddy died and she was too sick to keep it up. I inherited it when she died, but I just couldn't stay here in Dardanelle any more, so I closed it up and went off to the Army."

He fell silent, so she prompted him, "And then?"

"When I came back it was in even worse shape. I wanted to fix it up, for her if nothing else, but I just couldn't focus. It was Michael who got me started. He put me on a serious physical workout regimen. I agreed to let the house go for awhile and work on the outside. I needed lots of space, so he suggested that I not even sleep inside. That camp down on the creek saved my sanity. I started on the inside last fall. Just a few days now and then. It took me two months to get all that paper up!"

"By yourself?"

"Yep."

"I take it crawling around on ladders doesn't bother you."

"Nah. I climbed many a shaky building when I was in Afghanistan. Climbing something fixed into place is a real treat."

They moved through a short hall into a modern kitchen. Here the cabinets, walls, and fixtures needed work. He explained what he planned to do to restore the wood on the cabinets and showed her a picture of the new ceiling fixtures he had ordered from an antique dealer in Columbia, Missouri. She noticed a magnificent airplane plant and a sweet potato vine on the window ledge behind the sink. She liked the fact that he had a nurturing nature.

Lunch was ham salad sandwiches on whole wheat, fruit cups, chips and brownies he had baked himself. They chatted about happenings around Dardanelle, but stayed away from Michael's murder which she really couldn't discuss with him. But she had one related piece of information.

She told him about the DNA tests that showed that Michael had a daughter. Dewey looked at her hard as he figured out the implications. "That means I have a niece. How did you get her DNA? She's not in the criminal data base is she?"

"Hardly. She's a young lady who actually works at the forensic lab at MNSU. That's why her prints are in the data base--for exclusion since she handles a lot of samples."

"She's not doing this one is she? That might make it a conflict of interest and mess up trial testimony."

"No, no. Hattie West had already excluded her from the investigation because she was one of Michael's patients. This other came up later."

He rested his chin on the back of his hand and appeared to be in deep thought. "You reckon I can meet her?"

"Sure," she nodded. "I can set it up this week. I think she'd like to meet you too."

If Dewey were uncomfortable with having a surprise niece, he didn't show it. After lunch, he gathered up some fishing gear, a Styrofoam box from the fridge, and a couple of water bottles and they headed down a tiny trail west of the house. They were close to the part of Lake Dardanelle that ran beside Hwy-22. There were numerous creeks and small sloughs that merged with the lake further north. Sophia was beginning to wonder if he was trying to get her lost when they came to an opening with a small boat tied to a big catalpa tree.

Dewey unlocked the chain and pushed the boat into what appeared to be a shallow pond. He helped her get in then followed. There was no motor, but it didn't take him long to paddle along the bank into deeper water that disappeared around the corner. "This runs on into Elkins creek that empties into another creek, and so on, until it gets to the lake," he explained. "Now if you want bass, you need to go out to the lake. But if you want pan fish, this here's some of the best fishing you'll get.

"You like to cast, or do you want a bobber?" he was setting up the poles.

"I like to cast, with a bobber," she answered.

"OK, there ya go," he handed her a pole ready with hook, sinkers, and a bobber. "All I brought is worms. You want me to bait it for you?"

"No," she smiled. "I can do it myself. I went into a bait shop once to get some worms. The old goober sitting there says to me, 'Lady, you got someone ta put them on fer you?' So I looked at him, all wide eyed and innocent like, and I said, you mean they don't crawl on by themselves?" She worked the worm onto her hook and cast it out several yards from the boat.

The water was still pretty cold out in the lake, but here where it was relatively shallow, fish were starting to bite. In a little over an hour, between the two of them, they caught and released six nice size blue gill. They floated lazily down the stream until the boat pushed up against a bank.

Dewey checked his watch. "Guess it's time to head back in. It's still gettin' cold fast in the evenings. We can come back later when it's warmer. Once you finish this investigation, you'll have more time, and we'll keep our fish and fry them up fresh."

It's a deal," she nodded her head. "Unfortunately this investigation is wearing me down already. But I still have some leads to follow. Your brother knew a lot of people." She couldn't tell him more than that.

As they trekked back up the path to the house, she noticed leaves coming out on the brambles along the way. In another two or three weeks, you'd need a weed eater to get through here. The yard behind the house was covered in spring beauties, and here and there, a buttercup lifted its head. It would be easy to fall in love with this place.

—␣ᗯ␣—

On the way back into town, Dewey broached the subject of his newly found niece. "What can ya tell me about her?"

"Well," Sophia tried to be discreet, "her name is Bennie Sue Webb. She's 24 years old, she's a graduate of MNSU, and she works as a Certified Identity Specialist at the crime lab. She knows about you, that you're her uncle, that is. But I asked her not to make any contact until I could eliminate you as a suspect."

"Didn't want me to bump her off too?"

"Exactly." She made no excuses.

"Lady, you are nothing else if not honest," he was amused.

"It's my job. I can't go exposing sweet young things to ornery old vets unless I'm sure it's safe," she countered.

"Well, I'm pretty much free this week. If you can work it into your schedule, set up a meeting."

33

Sophia didn't think she'd ever have time to work a meeting into her schedule. The murder investigation wasn't going well. Here they were in the second week since Dintleman's death, and they were still chasing down leads. Dintleman knew too many people, and right now most of them qualified as suspects.

Her week was further complicated by the arrest of not one, but two, sex offenders for failure to register. One was a moderate risk offender who had failed to register once before. When Yell County officers and a U.S. Marshall had failed to locate him during a compliance check, the search was on. Failure to register could lead to a Class C felony. The second offender was designated as high risk. He too, was not where he was supposed to be. Authorities finally found him working at the food court in the Student Center at MNSU.

Just on a hunch, Sophia had her crew look at the car registration for Emily Leonard's father. One of the girls at the sorority had mentioned that Emily needed therapy to deal with her father. When the search showed that he owned a black

Infinity QX-15, Sophia perked up. Although it was unlikely, there was a possibility that he objected to her dating the football star or Michael Dintleman, and he blamed Dintleman for encouraging her. If so, J'Dane Warford could be in danger too.

She picked up her phone and called Joseph Long at the Springdale Police Department. After the requisite pleasantries, she explained her problem. "Look, Joe, this is probably a wild hair, but I need you to do some checking for me. You're aware of the Dintleman murder down here?" When he said he was, she continued. "Well, it turns out that Emerson Leonard's daughter was in a relationship with the good doctor. And, a big black SUV was seen down the Hollow just after the murder. And Emerson Leonard owns a black SUV, and..."

"OK, I get it," Joe responded. "Yeah, you're probably wrong. Leonard is snooty as hell, but he has a reputation for being an honest attorney. He's also one of our Blue Line supporters. Contributed quite a bit last year. I can't see him doing anything like that. What time do you need me to check for an alibi?"

She gave him the times, and he promised to call back when he had some information. She was really surprised when he called back within the hour.

"Sophia? Joe here. I have some good news and some bad news. Leonard says he has an alibi, but he won't talk to me. He wants to talk to you."

"You're kidding."

"Nope. He says to call his office to set up an appointment. He'll treat for lunch any day this week that you can come, just come in plain clothes, no uniform." He gave her the office number, gossiped a little about what the deal might be, and hung up.

Sophia called the number and made an appointment for lunch Thursday. She had a good idea what the problem was. Leonard had been somewhere that Sunday night that would look bad for him politically. He'd rather tell her directly than to have the local police find out and leak it. Oh, well, at least she'd get lunch out of it.

Meanwhile, Sophia called Bennie Sue to try to set up a meeting between her and Dewey. Bennie Sue suggested lunch Wednesday, or dinner Thursday. Since Sophia didn't know for sure where she'd be by Thursday, or what she might need to finish up then, she picked Wednesday lunch then called Dewey. He thought lunch was a great idea and insisted he treat. They agreed to meet at Tubs of Subs downtown.

Sophia spent the rest of her day trying to identify people to interview and to see how those already interviewed fit into the established timeline. She called Dr. Russell and left a message for a call-back. There were still some questions about the research project that needed clarification. He called back at 5:00 just as the day was winding down. He apologized for his lateness, explaining that he had picked up one of Dintleman's MWF afternoon classes. He sounded a little hassled and suggested, since they both had to eat, that they meet at Tarasco's Mexican at 6:30.

He even looked hassled when he came through the door and sat down across from her. His first order of business was to request a Margarita. Happy hour would not be wasted. He took a deep breath, but didn't seem to relax. So much for his psychology training. "What can I do for the Police Department?" he asked unenthusiastically.

"I need to ask you a few more questions about your research," she answered. You mentioned that some of the men decided to go into counseling? Was that a common thing?"

"Not particularly. Most men who are into porn are not seeking someone else's approval, and, quite frankly, they don't see any need for intervention. Still, there are a few, more than likely married men, who are just a little ashamed of their obsession, especially if their wives disapprove."

"Might there be some who would go to Dr. Dintleman, but resent what they perceived as disapproval?"

"I seriously doubt that. Michael was not judgmental with his patients. His method was to have the client, himself, identify why he felt distressed about the activity and whether he accepted or rejected his own desires. If he rejected his own behavior, Michael would help him work toward resolution. If he accepted it, wave goodbye."

"Did he ever deal with pedophiles?"

"No way! He had a real thing about that. He told his patients up front that he would have to report them to the police if he knew they had hurt a child sexually or been involved with child pornography. I'm guessing some of his porn addicts were also pedophiles, but not many. Different strokes for different folks, so to speak."

"But if a patient was hiding pedophilia, would Dintleman have figured it out?"

"I doubt it. It would have to come up some way during therapy for a different, if related, issue. Why do you keep asking?"

"I'm exploring the possibility that one of Dr, Dintleman's patients may have been angry enough or scared enough to silence him."

"Well, I wouldn't look at pedophilia. A real pedophile would get rid of all the evidence if he had any inkling he had been discovered. Some of these guys are super paranoid. They're looking for a cop around every corner. No, anger is a better track to take. Lots of people carry immense anger inside. You know it yourself. A little domestic violence mixed with a little liquor can produce a major explosion."

"You're right about that. I hated domestic calls before I bccame a detective. They'll kill each other tonight, that is until they decide to kill you for interfering with them. I never went to a domestic call alone. Sometimes two of us couldn't do the job."

"Did you ever sense that you might be breaking up a family that could have made it otherwise?"

"Not really. Adults who are that dysfunctional need to be separated. Chances are they'll find someone else of the same "religion" and get along until they don't. But kids deserve better than that. I don't understand everything that happens to a kids brain, but I think all that chaos and fighting has to affect them somehow."

"Yes, it apparently does. Several studies have come out in the past year or so verifying what we already knew but didn't have any data on. You have to have data for anything to be valid, even if it's sitting in front of you, you know. We used to think that because the brain is pretty elastic up until nine or ten that kids muddle through trauma in their lives without many bad side effects. Now we know they may carry scars for the rest of their lives."

"Yes," she agreed, "just like we've known for years that alcohol increases driving accidents and fatalities. But no one wanted to challenge dysfunctional drinkers no matter how much trauma they caused. We even let the alcoholics write the rules, just like we've let abusive parents write the rules. Look how long it took us to set a reasonable limit for intoxication and manufacture tools accurate enough to test it."

34

Sophia dressed up a little bit the next morning in preparation for her meeting with Attorney Leonard. She picked a neutral untailored jacket to which she added a bright scarf and matching earrings. She even wore low-heeled pumps, something she rarely did unless she was going to court (well, considering Leonard's reputation, maybe she was, just a little bit). She didn't want the lawyer to think she was a complete hick just because she lived in a poorer area of the state.

She called the office to pick up her messages and give a few directions on current cases. Then she headed up to I-40 on her way to I-540, Fayetteville, and Springdale. She made good time and arrived a little early. If she were pushing her timeline, she often got frustrated and spoke in curt sentences (something to keep working on to make herself a better person).

Emerson Leonard was not what she had expected. His daughter was snooty, and Sophia's friend, Joe, had described the father as snooty, but competent. He was wearing very expensive pleated kaki pants, and an unstructured navy jacket with an open-collared checked shirt. He wore dark socks and oxblood loafers. Clearly he was not planning to be in court today.

The attorney flashed a wide smile and held out his hand in greeting. "Let's go to my office for just a little while. Then I promise you a business-free lunch," he offered.

Surprisingly, there wasn't the requisite deep pile carpet. Instead bamboo flooring with a soft gloss had been laid in the hall and in his office. When she commented on it, he explained that allergies were a major concern to members of the firm with some employees requiring HEP filters. She wondered what she'd have to do to get HEP filters in the Dardanelle Police Department offices.

His office was cerulean blue with white blinds at the extra wide windows. His various degrees were displayed tastefully on the wall behind his chair, intended to assure the client of high standards. The other walls had enlarged photographs of the Buffalo River, Mt. Magazine, and old barns during different seasons. All-in-all, it was very calming and reminded her of Dr. Dintleman's office. Maybe some blue in her office would help calm her visitors down, that and the HEP filters.

"The reason I wanted to talk to you in person," he started, "is that our law enforcement in this area is notorious for leaks. You'd think this the White House! I also wanted to meet the person who is leading the investigation in case my daughter has to testify later. I am well aware that her sexual liaison with the good doctor, and with the football player, and God only knows who else, may cause her some difficulty later. I only hope her indiscretions don't bite her in the tail (he smiled at his own joke) later."

"So far, Emily," Sophia stated just as calmly, wondering how he could be so blasé about his own daughter's sexual activities, " has been cooperative. I can't comment on any other aspects of the investigation. She mentioned that she had spoken to you before coming in for an interview. I trust that she'll keep that line of communication open."

"Well spoken," he chuckled. "You're not likely to leak any gossip to outsiders."

"I appreciate the compliment," she pushed on, "and I hope you'll understand that our investigation requires knowledge of your whereabouts the Sunday evening Dr. Dintleman was murdered."

"Hmm," he put his hand on his mouth and pursed his lips. "This is a little indelicate, but I was at a cabin in Eureka Springs. I often take a half day off on Mondays and stay overnight somewhere on Sundays. And, yes, I was with someone. I'll give you the number for the cabins," he flipped through his rolodex. "You can verify that I was there."

Lunch was great. They went to a little out of the way oriental place where they both had honey-walnut shrimp to die for. They chatted about how police work and court cases dovetailed. He did divorces mainly, but kept his eye on criminal defense. He admitted that he didn't always feel comfortable representing some of his clients, but he'd never been a go-for-the-throat guy, so many of the divorces he handled were resolved without undue rancor. On the other hand...

She confided her frustration with having to train, then retrain young officers on protocol. It took a few of them seemingly forever to learn that botching up a crime scene could result in a perp going free.

When he dropped her back at her car, the first thing she did was call her office to have Donny check on Leonard's alibi. Better she "recuse" herself from that task considering she had just been wined and dined by the subject in question.

When Sophia returned to the office, Donny had left her a message: "Found something interesting. Should be back by 4:00." Meanwhile she had seemingly hundreds of things to attend to.

She had already spent almost 10 days on the Dintleman case with no real results. She needed to sit down with Donny and brainstorm. There had to be another avenue of interest.

On the surface, the man was clean. Sexually active, granted, but highly transparent. There had to be something or someone else in his life.

While she was muddling the Dintleman delimma, Donny popped into her office with his news. He had verified that Emerson Leonard had indeed been at a cabin in Eureka Springs that Sunday night. In fact he had been at the getaway's restaurant most of the evening with his cabin mate, one of the hunky Razorback football players!

"So he's not upset with his daughter shagging a black football player from MNSU because he's into the same game," Sophia surmised.

"Yes," Donny agreed. "But she's not trying to hide it. He is."

"Do you think Dintleman knew"

"I don't think it matters," he reasoned. "What matters is whether Leonard thought he knew, and wanted to keep it quiet. That area of the state is pretty liberal, but his clients may not be."

"Yeah, I see. But murder?"

"There's no telling what kinds of secrets a psychologist or psychiatrist may be keeping," Donny expounded. "If it's not illegal, he'll never tell. I guess we need to look at what kinds of secrets might lead someone to bludgeon him to death. We can't assume all his patients were rock solid citizens."

"Or," Sophia continued, "that they were all perfectly sane. We all know what border-liine personalities can do when they're really threatened. Oh my," she sighed, "I guess we'd better have a pretty good look at that list of patients we got from his billing records. I don't think this case is ever going to be over."

35

Bennie Sue was really nervous about the meeting tomorrow with Dewey Elkins. What if he hated her? What if he thought she was a fraud trying to get some of Michael's inheritance, although she had no idea how to go about that? What if? What if? What if?

She finally calmed herself by using the worst case scenario method Michael had taught her. What was the worst thing that could happen? One of them would reject the other after their meeting. What would that mean? It would mean they would go their respective ways and interact as little as possible with no big changes in either life. What if there really was an inheritance? It would mean she would have to get a lawyer and work through the legal system since she had no idea how inheritances worked. Meanwhile she was getting along fine without ever knowing that there might even be an inheritance. People kept asking her about a will, but it really wasn't any of their business.

What should she wear? Oh, no, she didn't have any new spring clothes! Then she calmed herself by asking one question: How do I want to present myself? She decided to approach the meeting as an interview, since in many ways it was. What would she wear for an interview? She picked out a professional looking jacket with a coordinated, not too frilly, blouse. She chose dark pants and one-inch heels with knee highs. She had worn an outfit like this to court on the few times she had testified about blood evidence. Since this wasn't a court appearance, she softened the outfit with pretty dangly earrings and a jade frog ring. A bangle watch would complete the outfit.

Wardrobe and attitude settled, Bennie Sue got comfortable on her little couch to watch a favorite cable program although her thoughts kept turning to her date with Jeff coming up this weekend. She slept well and arrived at the office early to get a few chores done before lunch.

—∿—

Dewey Elkins was restless too. Who is this girl? What if she doesn't like me? What if I don't like her? What if the subject of a will comes up? He finally calmed himself down by working through the scenarios the way Michael had taught him. What was the worst thing that could happen? They could hate each other. One of them would reject the other at first sight. What would that mean? It would mean they would go their respective ways and interact as little as possible with no big changes in either life. What if there really was an inheritance? It would mean she would have to get a lawyer and work through the legal system. He knew a little about Arkansas law from his mother's death. But she had a will. Did Michael? No one had found it yet. Meanwhile he was getting along with what he had. He didn't have to have Michael's inheritance.

Since this was an important meeting, he set out what he had worn to Michael's memorial, but with a different shirt and tie. He'd shower and change in the morning. Meanwhile he gathered a few things and walked out to his camp. The night sounds and the shadow of a moon would soothe his PTSD and let him sleep tonight.

The person who had the least to gain from tomorrow's meeting had the most trouble sleeping. Sophia didn't know why she was so nervous. It was the whole Dintleman-Elkins thing. It was 10 days since the murder, and the leads were freezing up. It had to be someone in the community who could get to know the doctor's Sunday evening patterns. The closest person physically, besides two neighbors who were gone, was Dewey. And Dewey had given them the presumed murder weapon. But she hadn't been able to convert that into a lead. And Dewey, what was she going to do about him? Was she looking for a relationship? She had plenty of failed ones. Was he looking for a relationship? How many failed ones did he have?

Sophia's thoughts finally wandered back to Bennie Sue. Yikes! That girl had a patchwork past. Her father was in prison for molesting her and showing her his child pornography. Her Aunt Alexis's husband had moved out not too long after Bennie Sue joined their family. And now, a man she apparently trusted had been murdered. It might not be to Bennie Sue's advantage to introduce another man into her life, especially one with vague family connections.

Her mind bounced back to the murder case. She knew she needed to put it away so the back burner in her mind could sort and simmer. She finally decided that her plan tomorrow would be to start looking at the list of Dintleman's patients. Who might have an issue that was worth killing for?

36

Sophia left for lunch early. She wanted to get there in time to make the introductions. She didn't want any awkward standing around. When she parked outside Tubs of Subs, she spotted Bennie Sue parked four slots down. Evidently she wanted to get there in time to see Dewey go into the sub house. But, when they entered together, Dewey was already seated at a table toward the back slowly drinking his coffee. Not anxious a bit, these three!

Sophia led Bennie Sue to the back of the room and introduced her to Dewey who actually rose from his chair. If Bennie Sue was not impressed by this, she was going to be a hard sell. Sophia went to the front to put in their orders, leaving the two of them alone.

"I saw you at the memorial," Bennie Sue offered.

"And I saw you," he returned. "You were sitting in the back. To repeat an old cliché, I would have known you anywhere. The resemblance to Michael is quite strong. I didn't know who you were at the time (Sophia's been pretty crafty about this), but I remember you."

"You're very observant," Bennie Sue compli-mented him. "I work for the State Crime Lab where we look at everything in minute detail. I'm always amazed at what people don't see. Thanks to you, we have what we believe to be the murder weapon. I'm glad Sophia managed to eliminate you from our suspects list."

37

The trail of Evelyn Goodson, the student who had lived with Dintleman while she was pregnant, her lover, and her ex-husband had grown cold. There was little known about them after they hied off to Atlanta. However, there was a Wilson Goodson on the personal property rolls at the courthouse. Thursday afternoon Sophia took a break from the tiring task of finding nothing; She and Donny drove by Goodson's apartment about 6:00, hoping to catch him after work.

Wilson Goodson was obviously startled and somewhat taken aback by the lady detective and her uniformed sidekick standing at his door. "Can I help you?" he asked politely, knowing for certain that he hadn't done anything to bring the police around. Still, some of the neighbors were leery of two gay black men living nearby, and they could have reported something from their imaginations.

"Yes," she smiled reassuringly, "I'm trying to find an Evelyn Goodson."

At that he threw back his head and laughed out loud. "Oh, you are, are you? What has dear Evelyn

Goodson, or whatever she is calling herself now, got herself into this time?"

We wanted to talk to her, and to you, in reference to the Dintleman murder," Sophia was blunt. "May we come in?"

"Oh, yes. Yes." He moved aside to allow them to enter. Better to talk inside. Neighbors might wonder what they were doing out there on his doorstep. So far the neighbors had been cool about his living arrangements, but he was certain any number of them disapproved.

The apartment was neatly, if sparsely, furnished with the requisite flat screen TV and small couch and recliner. There were no pictures or other decorations on the walls, but the picture on a side table of two men wearing tuxedos embracing each other told its own story.

"Nice place," Sophia smiled as she and Donny took the couch with Wilson across from them in the recliner. "How long have you been here?"

"Just six months," Wilson responded. "We got married in the Dominican Republic in July then lived in Gary's old apartment in Russellville until we found this one. We both work for Harps, but we liked the ambience here better than in Dover."

"I bet you do," Sophia agreed. She could just imagine the trouble two married black men might encounter in the much smaller town.

"Weren't you in Atlanta?" she didn't waste any time. "I understand that you made some threats against Dr. Dintleman before following Ms. Goodson there."

Wilson looked down at his feet before meeting her eyes directly. "Yes, you're right. My wife was living with the man while she divorced me. I was convinced she was the only one for me and that Dintleman had encouraged her betrayal. I wanted to ring his neck. She was really pushing him to marry her. Then foop! She ran off with Mr. Whitaker! She had delivered the baby by the time I caught up with her, and I finally figured out what she had been up to."

"How so?"

"The baby was white. It wasn't my baby," he said, shaking his head. She was looking for a white man to marry while she was planning to sue me for child support. Well, you can imagine the relief. I turned right around and came back here. I actually went to Dintleman and thanked him for not marrying her. He just smiled and told me he knew all the time the baby wasn't his."

"So you parted with Dintleman on good terms?"

"Oh, yeah. That man saved me from all kinds of grief in the end. There was no reason at all for me to harm him."

38

Keith sat at his desk in the loans department and went over a spreadsheet of dates and numbers. It had been a good month so far. By tightening loan qualifications, the bank had virtually ensured that all their loans would fit into "bundles" to be sold to the giant mortgage companies.

He let his mind wander briefly, looking forward to tonight's business meeting in Conway. Area loan managers met every third Thursday at the Conway branch to go over recent results and to get briefings on expected changes in rates and/or requirements. Keith was not looking forward to that at all. While his accounts were always in order and clearly laid out, there were one or two managers who always gummed up the works and wasted time with their incompetence. His anticipation of the meeting-after-the-meeting would help reduce some of the teeth grinding. He had sent Seth a SanDisk earlier in the week, and he wanted to see the results.

Sometimes Keith took Cassie and Candie with him and let them shop while he went to his meeting. He'd pick them up afterwards and take them to dinner. Candie especially liked TGIF. But tonight, as he did from time to time, he had lied to Cassie that the meeting would be especially long and suggested that the girls stay in town and go to Braums for a sandwich and ice-cream. Cassie had seemed almost relieved. She'd been a little stand-offish lately. Probably just hormones.

As soon as the bank meeting was over, Keith used a burner phone to call Seth, and they agreed to meet at their usual place, Paddy's Pizza and Grill. These guys had stayed friends since university where they saw each other at frat parties and business classes. Keith had gone the harder route, taking an MBA in accounting and finance that had set him up for bank management. Seth had experimented with finding himself, usually in the embrace of an illegal substance. He had been in and out of rehabs several times and always swore he was done with his latest temptation. Fortunately his daddy was rich.

Seth had already ordered the large supreme "special". Keith was buying tonight and handed his friend a $100.00 prepaid Visa to cover the cost. When their order was ready, Seth passed the money across the counter. The cashier never blinked an eye. Scanned the Visa on the reader under the counter then rang up the price of the pizza and handed Seth a few small bills and some change. Then he passed the boxed "special" across the counter. The next customer in line paid for his pizza and took it back to his table to eat.

The two men drove in separate cars to Seth's apartment where he opened two beers and pulled the pizza out onto a serving platter. After they'd both downed two giant slices, Seth opened two more beers, and they got down to business. Under the cardboard circle was a 2-1/4 inch by 3-½ inch apple green cardstock envelope. Keith did the honors by peeling the protective plastic off and unsealing the envelope. Inside was a memory card for a digital camera.

Keith retrieved his digital camera from his briefcase and took the memory card from Seth. He popped it into the camera and began reviewing the photos.

The pictures were breathtaking. Pouty-mouthed young women with beautiful bodies were captured in all the poses that stoked a man's fantasy about sex in bed. There was one that was actually pretty funny. A woman lay with her legs spread apart displaying, not her vagina, but a life-like dildo of a man's penis and balls inserted backwards into her vagina--what a trip! Both men snickered at the absurdity.

Then Keith viewed the last picture, shot from the neck down. On the top, she wore a little pink bikini embroidered with rose buds. There were two small roses positioned over where the nipples were likely to be. On the bottom, she was naked. Here a pink silk rose was positioned on her pelvis just above the little labia visible between her spread legs.

"She's beautiful," Keith declared softly, stroking the labia gently.

"Oh, yeah," Seth agreed. "Now you, you've got real talent. When can you get me some more of your little cunt?"

"Well," Keith hedged, "it's not all that easy."

"Oh, come on," Seth rejoined. "You've been taking pictures of that little sweetie for years now. She'll do whatever you ask her to do. You can pop that little cherry anytime you want to. You owe it to all her fans who've been sending you their stuff."

"Yeah, but she's getting bigger (Seth nodded lasciviously), and she's starting to get a little shy. Besides, what if she tells Cassie?"

"Then you handle it, Man. You handle it. Come on, you owe us. You know you do."

"How much are you getting for this stuff?" Keith wanted to know. He was reluctant to use his own pictures to bankroll Seth.

"Fifty dollars for the usual package; plus $25 for the kid."

"Can they buy them separately?"

"Only the usual package. You have to buy both to get the kid."

—◊—

Driving back to Russellville, Keith was conflicted. He didn't like where this thing with Seth was going. Keith loved pornography because it made him feel horney and masculine. The kiddy porn was more like a sweet dream with the promise of more to come. He sensed that Seth had a very different perspective. Seth's choice of photos was getting increasingly more violent. Seth seemed to need stronger stimulus centering around pain. Keith couldn't imagine sticking something up Candie's rear just to turn Seth on. He didn't know where Seth got some of the disgusting photos of little kids having sex with each other and posing with various objects protruding from their orifices; no way did those depictions suggest sweet dreams. Keith was a good man and a good father. He would never participate in something so disgusting! And yet...

Keith didn't stay on his high horse very long. He had learned during therapy with Michael Dintleman how to be honest with himself. He had gone to Dintleman almost a year ago when his obsession with porn was re-blossoming just as it had before Candie was born. He had admitted his heightened feelings of masculinity when he saw porn. He had practiced moving his thoughts to other pathways. He practiced visualizing himself doing something masculine without the aid of porn. His sex life with Cassie had improved, and he felt he was finally on his way.

What happened? Seth Gunter happened. They were frat brothers at Tau Tau Tau some years ago whern Seth introduced Keith to the truly raunchy side of sex. From popping cherries at frat parties to visiting brothels, Seth knew all the ins and outs, so to speak. Keith was pursuing a double major in Mathematics and Management & Marketing. Seth was majoring in debauchery. He kept his grades just high enough to keep from being kicked out and therefore losing Daddy's generous gravy train. But Keith couldn't remember for the life of him what Seth's major was.

Keith got behind during his junior year when he contracted Mono and ended up dropping most of his courses during the fall semester. When his mind finally cleared and a little stamina returned, he was way behind. He ended up taking summer courses and signed up for an extra load of special topics during the first semester of his senior year. Seth had disappeared during the summer, and Keith was too busy actually putting his nose to the grindstone to miss him much. But Seth kept showing up at the frat house for parties, and they parted good friends.

The good friend thing continued during the next several years of Keith's life: wedding, job promotions, new house, new baby, Little Miss pageants. Seth might show up at anytime, always well heeled and seemingly happy. Then Keith heard via an old frat brother that Seth was doing some time for sex with an underage girl. Seth's daddy got the sentence reduced with a plea deal, but Seth still had to register as a sex offender. Seth treated his sentencing deal as a mere inconvenience and frequently "forgot" to register as he moved about the state. Based on Seth's comments last weekend, Keith would have bet good money that Seth was out of compliance now.

39

The Friday lunch this week turned into a celebration of sorts. Cathy Torres of Benton County had accepted a sentence of life without parole in return for her admission of guilt in her six year old son's death. This put an end to a horrifying case of child abuse that had been in the courts for two years. Two years ago Maurice Isaiah Torres had been brought to the hospital in Bella Vista in battered and non-responsive condition. The boy died from an internal infection caused by rupture of his colon. Investigators discovered that Isaiah had been his father's punching bag for years. Bruises and scars from beatings covered his emaciated body, and x-rays revealed broken and partially healed bones that had never been treated. While these injuries were contributing factors to his death, Isaiah had died from an infection caused when his father pushed a stick up his rectum and punctured his intestines. His mother had been present at the campsite and reportedly pushed Isaiah down on the stick because she was angry with him.

The father, Mauricio Torres had pleaded innocent and had gone to trial in November. He was convicted and sentenced to death by lethal injection. Looking at a probable repeat when she came to trial, Cathy Torres had taken a plea deal just before her scheduled March trial.

"Can you imagine pleading innocent to something like that?" Garnet was incredulous.

"Yeah, of course he was innocent, just like that guy who claimed his cat had downloaded thousands of images of child pornography," Rachel scoffed. She was just thankful that she hadn't had to perform the postmortem on the little boy. Abused children gave her nightmares.

"There's an awful lot of that going on," Bennie Sue offered. "I keep a file of child abuse articles from newspapers and internet each year. My files are very thick."

"We're sorry, Dear," Hattie patted her hand on the table. "All this death must be really hard for you. But at least things are looking up."

"Yes, Bennie Sue," Garnet pried, changing the subject, "when are you going to tell us about your new uncle? Did anything, or anybody, I should say, turn up in your genealogy search?"

"No, he's the only one so far," Bennie Sue answered the second question. "And I can tell you that I really liked him when we met Wednesday. Sophia put us together for lunch. We just chatted and exchanged phone numbers. I'll call him early next week to set up another meeting. Sooner or later we'll have to get down to brass tacks about the estate. But I really want to take it easy for now."

"A little bird told me Sophia and Dewey might have a little thing going," Hattie gossiped. "What's your take on it?"

Bennie Sue chuckled as she responded. "Yeah, that could be. I thought I saw a little spark there, especially when he called her back when we were leaving. We'll just have to get her to come to lunch with us when she can. That way we can get the goods straight out."

"I'll call her," Garnet agreed. "Meanwhile you had better be our spy!"

"Speaking of sparks," Rachel joined in, "when are you going to be seeing Jeff again?"

"How did you know?"

"He misdialed by one number. Since I couldn't transfer him, I talked to him. He seems like a good natured sort."

"Yeah," Bennie Sue agreed. "As a matter of fact, I'm going over to Conway tonight. It's St. Patty's Day, and we're going to drink some green beer."

40

Green beer was already flowing when Bennie Sue arrived at Jeff's apartment. He, his roommate, and several men and women from his physical therapy classes were watching the first round of March Madness, guzzling beer, and scarffing up chips and dips. Jeff introduced Bennie Sue around then continued taking pizza orders. The plan was to call in to Paddy's Pizza and Grill then make a mad dash to pick them up at half time. Just before half time everybody shelled out cash, and Jeff and Bennie Sue were ready to go.

Paddy's was pandemonium. They had to park a block away on the outside edge of a grocery lot. Arkansas was in the tournament, and had made it through the first round, so some of the loyal fans were calling the hogs. All the tables were taken, and there was a long line at the pickup counter. By the time they wedged their way up to the cashier, half time was nearly over. "Order for Jeff", he shouted. The cashier turned toward the stacks of takeout on the shelf behind him and finally located the order. Cash was most welcome. The chip reader on the

credit card machine was malfunctioning, and customers had to learn which direction to turn a card
to swipe it and how to sign a piece of paper all over
again.

By the time the Salt Lake City games came on,
all the pizza, cake, cookies, corn dogs, etc. had
been decimated. But there was still plenty of beer.
Bennie Sue took a break just to get up and stretch
and began gathering the trash. One of the pizza
boxes had something stuck under the cardboard
circle. She had no idea what it was. It was just a little green envelope with some numbers printed on
the bottom. Maybe it was a prize of some sort. She
washed the pizza sauce off her hands and opened
it. Inside was a SanDisk like the one in her digital
camera. She knew it was odd, but she wasn't thinking too clearly by now, so she stuffed it down into
the back pocket of her jeans and immediately forgot about it because Jeff came by just then and gave
her one of his soft kisses.

Bennie Sue was ambivalent about staying the
night. Part of her wanted to, but another part was
waving red flags. The first part had packed a duffle
with jammies and a change of clothes just in case
she stayed. It was still out in her car just in case
she didn't. Jeff's roommate grabbed his duffle and
headed out with one of the women in the group. By
the time everyone else had cleared out, it was just
Bennie Sue and Jeff.

"Well, I guess I'd better be heading back too,"
Bennie Sue offered.

"No way," he responded. "You're probably not safe on the highway. Besides, I'm afraid to stay alone." By now he had his arms around her.

She leaned against him and looked down into the deep, deep well of her own emotions. Throwing the flags aside, she surprised herself. "I was hoping you would ask."

—◦◦◦—

As soon as she got home Saturday, Bennie Sue started piling clothes into the washer. After an Egg McMuffin breakfast and lots of coffee, she had begged off of an afternoon of NCAA basketball. She needed time to herself. As she was putting a load of darks in, she remembered the envelope in her jeans. Better not to wash that disk. She laid the envelope on her small kitchen table and went to hunt up her digital camera. Digital cameras were going out of style now that people used their phones for pictures.

As she flipped through the pictures, she was disgusted. It was PORN! She continued advancing the pictures just in case there was a hidden message somewhere. Toward the end of the sequence, she caught her breath. There on her camera were three little girls parading in their mother's clothes. Another little girl appeared dressed in a black lacy slip that slid off her shoulders exposing her nipples. *That's me! We were at Beth Ann's trying on her mother's lingerie.* Then there was a picture of three little girls sitting naked on the edge of a Jacuzzi with handfuls of soap bubbles sliding off their pre-pubescent breasts and pubic areas. *Damn! I took that picture. These must have been on that camera Beth Ann carried around with her all the time. But how did they get here? In a green envelope hidden under a pizza?*

Bennie Sue grabbed her phone and looked up an old number that she hadn't used for several years. Then she placed a call to Beth Ann in Conway. She got the business answering machine: "Beth Ann's Modeling and Photography is closed. Please call again during our regular business hours of 10:00 to 6:00 Monday through Thursday. You can leave a message at the tone."

Bennie Sue didn't have Beth Ann's cell number so she left a message for a call back. Bennie Sue and Beth Ann had reconnected briefly from time to time. They had some mutual friends on Face Book, but were not close. Beth Ann's folks had moved closer to Springdale so her mom didn't have to drive so far. Beth Ann earned her degree in photo journalism from UofA then worked in California for a while before returning to the area to set up her own business. Bennie Sue figured Beth Ann had a silent partner since her equipment was cutting edge, and she bought property in a higher end part of the commercial district.

Bennie Sue had never known the name of the man who had set Beth Ann up to take pictures of her friends when they were little girls, but she thought Beth Ann needed to know that those photos were still in circulation. Bennie Sue wondered how many dirty old men and pedophile scum had seen those pictures. It wasn't fair! She had been a little girl, trying to grow up. She had been innocent, but somehow she still felt shame.

41

It was Monday morning before Beth Ann returned the call. Bennie Sue got right to the point, "I have some digital photos that you need to see. I can't talk about it over the phone. I can come to you. Just give me a time."

So OK, She's really in a dither, Beth Ann thought to herself. She checked her schedule and suggested 4:00 at the shop.

No one had ever really explained to Bennie Sue what had gone on that night Della hauled them all down to the police department. The adults were obviously upset, but they kept pretending everything was all right. Then Judge Matthews and Dr. Dintleman had decided she needed to be moved to Pottsville. It was still really fuzzy in her memory, but she knew that the pictures on that little SanDisc were the key to the puzzle.

Beth Ann's studio was small, but elegant. Polished wood floors, expensive pecan desk and credenza, pastel window treatments, real plants, and soft accent pottery created an aura of calm and competence. It was no wonder she was the photographer of choice for aspiring models, graduating seniors, and beauty queens. Some of her photos were displayed on one wall that she had set up as a gallery. Once you saw them, you'd want her to do one of you too.

When Bennie Sue entered, she heard a light jingle in the back of the studio. Beth Ann appeared and told her it would be about 15 minutes. She offered Bennie Sue a cold beverage, then disappeared into the back where she was finishing a sitting for two-year old twins. Bennie Sue sipped her peach tea and waited until the twins and their proud mother were finally out the door.

"OK, what's the big emergency?" Beth Ann wanted to know.

Bennie Sue answered by pulling the disc out of its green envelope and loading it into her camera. "There are some photos here I think you need to see." She handed the camera to Beth Ann.

Beth Ann scanned through the porn at the front of the disc. She was very blasé about the contents. "So what? It's just porn. You can get it anywhere."

"Keep going," Bennie instructed. "There's more."

"When Beth Ann saw the child porn photos, her whole attitude changed. "What the..." she started. Then she came to the photos of the little girls taken years ago. "I can't believe this! That's us! That son of a bitch..."

"I thought you'd be interested," Bennie Sue interjected. "I couldn't believe it either. Now I know why they say that child pornography victimizes the child twice. I know we were just innocents, but somehow I still fell shame when I look at the photos."

Shame was not what Beth Ann was feeling. Absolute fury crossed her brain. "What are you going to do with these?"

"I thought I'd take them to Detective Cash over in Clarksville. He's still there, and he'll remember them from when we were kids. He'll know who took them and set a search in motion."

Beth Ann knew who it was too. And she knew where to find him, but she didn't breath a word of it to Bennie Sue. "Yeah, I think that's the best idea. Just be careful you're not blamed for possession. Thanks for the 'heads-up'. I'll feel better when they catch the bastard. Let me know how it goes."

42

Keith Kelly was driving down West Main in Russellville on Monday, headed to one of the branch banks, when he caught sight of Cassie's little Juke at one of the doctors' complexes. He made a right turn at the next corner and circled the block to investigate. She hadn't said anything about a doctor's appointment this week, and he wondered what she was up to. He turned into the lot and cruised slowly past the various offices. She was just coming out of Dr. Frank Norton's office. *Norton, isn't he some kind of psychiatrist or something?* He quickly drove past and parked on the back side of the lot.

The panic attack was full blown. His hands were shaking, and he broke out all over with sweat. *She's going to leave me! She's going to leave me! She's going to leave me! It's just like with Dintleman. She's been working up her courage, and she's going to leave me and take Candie with her. Dintleman knew. He never said anything, but he knew. That's why he told me that pedophiles are almost impossible to cure, but he thought he could help me with the adult porn. I can't believe he'd actually have me wear a shock collar to wean me from the pretty little pictures. I don't think I could ever give them up. And now this Norton guy probably knows too. They're not taking Candie away from me. I've got to* stop *it!*

Keith had pretty well pulled himself together by the time he got home around 6:00. He'd worked out his plan by then, and he was determined that Cassie would never catch on. She was in the kitchen, and Candie was in her bedroom, so he nonchalantly strolled back to his office. Closing the door, he took out his desk key and opened the drawer. Everything looked perfectly normal. The flash stick was where he had left it with the edge on the back square of the graph paper, and the memory discs from the camera were still under the felt pad in his Mont Blanc pen set. Whew! What a relief. No need to be paranoid. Maybe she didn't know everything after all.

He locked the drawer and went down the hall to get a big hug from his girl. Then he walked back to the kitchen with a good bit of resolve. It wasn't too late yet.

Keith walked up behind Cassie and put his arms around her, kissing the back of her neck. "Hey, how's my favorite girl? How's your depression been? I thought I saw your car at the doctors' complex today," he feigned affection.

Cassie wasn't sure what to think, knowing from experience that he was fishing for something, but his touch felt so good that she played along. Leaning back into him, she answered. "Your favorite girl is doing just fine. I went to see Dr. Norton today," she cut him off at the pass. "He says I'm getting lots better. Things really are starting to look brighter again."

"That's great, Hon. I tell you what. Let's celebrate. Let's go out for dinner."

She wanted to say no. She would normally have made an excuse about wasting food or being too tired. But she marshaled some of her inner resources and agreed. "All right! You don't have to make that offer twice."

As she went down the hall to their bedroom to comb her hair and put on lipstick, she passed his office, knowing the evil that lurked there. She had to appear normal or he would know she was on to him. She rounded Candie up and headed back to the front of the house.

"Where would you like to go?" she asked tentatively, fully prepared to be outnumbered.

Candie spoke up immediately, I want to go to Steak and Shake in Russellville. They have neat hats for kids to wear."

To her surprise, Cassie heard Keith say, "No. Let's go where Mommy wants to go tonight. She doesn't get to choose very often. We'll go to Steak and Shake next time."

"You want to go to Steak and Shake too, don't you? Candie wheedled, sure Mommy would give in and she would get her way with Daddy as usual.

"No, I don't think so," Cassie pushed her luck, secretly putting another test in front of Keith. "Let's go to Catfish Boogie. I'm hungry for catfish and hushpuppies, and you love their popcorn shrimp, don't you, Punkin?"

"Yeah, yeah!" Candie clapped her hands together. "Catfish Boogie, Catfish Boogie!"

Keith was pleased with their dinner choice. The fish house had been open a short time and was still a good place to go. It was located down by the river just south of Clarksville. With Candie sitting between them in the front seat of the big SUV chattering during the entire 40 minute drive there and back, there was little need to interact with Cassie.

On the way home, Cassie pretended to doze off while Candie chattered. Keith half listened as he felt his mind scanning the back roads of his memory looking for specific images. He teased himself thinking first he could look at this one, then maybe that one, etc. The nearer to the house, the quicker his breathing came as he anticipated a private session in his office.

After they got home, Keith wrestled with Candie for a while then tucked her into bed. He kissed Cassie on the cheek and told her again how happy he was that she had perked up. Then he made the excuse of bank work and locked himself into his office. He opened the drawer, but did not remove the memory stick. Instead, he lifted the felt base of his pen set and took out one of the memory discs and popped it into his camera. He moved from disc to disc savoring the images that Seth had recorded for him. He thought finally about how Seth was becoming more insistent that he shoot and share some more pictures of "Candie's little cunt". What could he set up that would make everybody jealous of his little treasure trove? He was scheduled to meet Seth after his bank meeting next Thursday. Better get on it. She was getting shyer as she got a little older. Perfectly normal, but not at all helpful. What was he going to get her to do?

—◊—

Cassie, too, had been relieved by the child's chatter and the table of chattering friends tonight. She had practiced counting four-beat breathing to keep herself calm as she reviewed the day's business in her mind. She had her first meeting with Dr. Norton last week. After Dr. Dintleman's death, he had offered to take as many of the dead doctor's patients as possible. Cassie had jumped at the chance. She had worked with Dintleman enough to know that she needed to, wanted to, had to, get out of her marriage. She confided in Dr. Norton from the first apppointment and impressed on him how Keith's obsessive behavior with his porn, and now his daughter too, had eroded her trust. She wasn't asking for permission any more. She was determined to leave the marriage! What she did not tell Norton, and indeed, could hardly admit even to herself, was what she had found in Keith's drawer.

He had slipped the sacred key off his key ring last week and had left it in his suit pocket. She had found it when she was getting his clothes ready to

take to the cleaner's. At first she didn't think anything of it. Then it dawned on her just what it was.
Trembling and watching the door lest he surprise
her, she had ever so slowly opened the drawer,
being sure to mark the direction of the keyhole so
she could return it to the correct position. Inside,
all she saw was a memory stick and a set of Mont
Blanc pens. As carefully as she had examined the
position of the keyhole, she noted the stick's position with one corner lined up with two sides of a
piece of graph paper and the printing on the stick
face down.

Cassie quicky grasped the edges of the stick with
a tissue, paranoid that Keith would somehow be
checking for fingerprints. She ran to her own computer where she copied the entire drive as quickly
as her shaking hands would allow. She was afraid
that if she opened the stick on Keith's computer
he would know somehow. She replaced the stick,
turned the lock to just the right place and dropped
the key back into his suit pocket. That night she'd
mentioned plans to go to the cleaner's tomorrow so
he'd have time to retrieve the key.

The next day when she gathered the suit once
again, the key was gone. So far she was safe. She
waited until Candie was gone to a play date to open
the files. They were exactly what she had expected,
all kinds of pornographic images. So what was the
big secret? They'd been down this ugly path before.
He had sworn to stop, and she had pretended he
believe him.

It was the last pic on the last file to be opened that stopped her cold. It was a picture of a little girl in a pink bikini with embroidered roses. Cassie recognized it immediately. She was the one who had sewn those roses on! The little girl's bottom was naked, and a silk rose lay over her little pubic bone just above the little labia exposed by her widely spread legs!

Cassie went to their bedroom and grasped the silk rose in its bud vase. She flung it across the room, but her rage was not sated. She marched down the hall to Candie's room and retrieved the second rose. *How could he?* Candie was so proud of that rose. Keith had been so much nicer lately, and now Cassie knew why. She carried the two roses out to the garage where she picked up the pruning scissors and a small shovel. In the back yard she hastily dug a shallow grave for the roses which she snipped into tiny pieces and stomped into the ground, wishing she could stomp Keith instead.

Cassie removed the stick and turned off her computer. She sat in her chair and shook as if her whole world were rattling. Then she gritted her teeth, stood up, squared her shoulders and walked resolutely to the utility room where she buried the stick in a box of laundry detergent.

43

Tuesday morning while Bennie Sue was delivering the telltale disc to the Clarksville police, Seth Gunter was headed for Delilah's studio. A sweet young thing was meeting him there for a photo shoot. With any luck, he could work it into something more.

Seth didn't understand why his key wasn't working. He tried it several times then began banging on the door. "Delilah, are you in there? My key won't work."

"Sorry about that," she apologized as she let him in. "I had to have the locks changed to keep the riff-raff out. You know how it is."

Something in her tone warned him. "Sure, sure, whatever works for you. Care to give me a copy of the new key?"

"No, sir, you will not get a key and you will never come to this studio again!" Her voice was trembling with rage. "You promised me you were not doing child porn, and I was stupid enough to believe you!"

"Hey, Babe," he tried to talk her down, "I'm out of that stuff like I told you. Where'd you get the idea I was still doing kids?"

"A little messenger brought me a green envelope. And what should it contain? A SanDisc. And what should be on it? Pictures of some little girls that used to live in Clarksville. You lying scum!"

"Now, now," he held up his hands to show his palms, trying to placate her, "I can explain. Yes, I circulated those pictures, but that was years ago. Someone else must be using them. Besides, no one will know it was you." He was all innocence.

"Don't lie to me! I know all about your clever little scheme to sell porn with pizzas. You're the only one using those green envelopes. And this one had child porn in it!"

"Well, well, aren't we the self-righteous one?" His tone was menacing now. "Who taught you how to use a camera? Who pushed you into this line of work? And who lent you the money to set up this studio? You were just a wannabe little punk when I found you. You owe me a lot!"

"I don't owe you anything! How many times have you used this studio free? And how many times have you taken your cut of the films we did together?"

"I swear I didn't shoot any child porn here," he lied. "What business is it of yours what I do?"

"You screwed up. Two of those photos had my tell in them. There's a little marker on the bed that you missed," she lied to him. "You thought you were smart coming in when I was at the other studio."

"You bitch, don't you mess with me. I'll tell everybody who you really are! How do you think Beth Ann's Modeling and Photography will do when they find out you're Delilah Delight?"

"Don't threaten me, Seth. Those photos are at Clarksville right now. The clock is running. You better clear out and clear out fast. They know you're in Conway with your little green envelopes, and they know about Paddy's Pizza. They'll be on your tail like flies on dog shit. And don't you ever come back here! Besides," she spit out spitefully, "you never finished my portfolio!"

—⚏—

Seth had never known panic the way he knew panic now. He ran to the driveway and backed Delilah's old car out onto the street. Then he ran into the garage to get his own SUV. He still had paper tags on it which he knew would be easy to spot, so he opened the back and took out a set of stolen Texas plates. Texas required front and back plates. They'd be looking for the single Arkansas plate on the back. His fingers fumbled as he piled through his emergency kit for a screw driver. The screws on the front were stiff, and he cut himself on the plate trying to hold it in place and screw it on.

Gas! He needed gas. But gas stations had cameras. He pulled into an outside pump at a large station and filled up using his card. He kept his ball cap pulled down in front so he'd be hard to identify, especially with Texas plates. He drove out going north then turned back after two blocks and made a bee-line for his apartment. Maybe he'd throw them off; hopefully they'd concentrate on north-bound routes.

At his apartment, he cleared out everything, including his old, battered up microwave. As long as he had it he could start over anywhere. He hesitated over the box of green envelopes then stuffed them into his laundry basket. Before he went out the back he texted several of his colleagues, just to give them a heads-up. He hung his clothes on the pop-out rod and piled the rest of his stuff in the back. He was just another traveler coming home to Texas after a party weekend. He figured his best bet was to head for Texarkana. Fast moving vehicles on I-30 were commonplace, and there were likely to be fewer patrol cars out on a Tuesday.

—◆—

Delilah/Beth Ann, whoever she was, waited one hour. Then she called the tip line for the Conway police. "I have information about a sex offender, Seth Gunter. He's on his way out of the state right now. No I don't know where he's going. But if you catch the pedophile scum, check out his microwave very carefully."

44

Keith was still obsessing Tuesday morning about how well he was managing Cassie. He had just convinced himself (again) to give up on the Candie photos. So what if Seth was pissed with him? There were lots of photos out there. No need to add more of Candie.

He had mounds of paperwork to do today, but he paused to check for messages on his burner phone. His blood ran cold when he saw Seth's last message, *Going for a long run. Contact you later.*

Seth's situation had blown up! He was on the run! Seth had names and numbers for every pedophile and child pornographer in the state. What if Seth got caught? What if the police came here to question him? To say that his panic attack was full blown was putting it mildly. This one was much worse than yesterday's.

Keith began to feel unusually warm, almost as if he had a fever. The sweat popped out at his hairline followed by his underarms, and he shuddered as it began to trickle down his back. He checked the thermostat just in case then took his jacket off and loosened his tie. His embarrasment was acute when his secretary commented, "Oh, my, are you going for the casual look today?"

"No. Just have lots of paperwork today. Thought I'd get comfortable." He joked to himself that if he got any hotter, Al Gore was likely to show up.

He started reconciling ledgers and found his hands were shaking. Try as he might, he could not silence the nattering in his mind. *What if they come here? They'll drag me downstairs through the lobby in front of everyone! My name and photo will be in all the local papers. If they take me up to Russelllville, my mug shot will be in the paper there with all those criminals* (he had never convinced himself that what he had been doing was criminal).

His stomach started hurting, and he made frequent trips to the toilet as his bowels loosened in sympathy. *What if they come get me in the toilet?* He could just hear them, "Yeah, we caught the big asshole wiping his ass (and lots of laughter)."

Keith overcame some of his paranoia and walked down the street two blocks to Tubs of Subs for a late sub lunch. He was relieved that his shaking had stopped and he was finally getting a grip. He smiled at the cashier and gave his order. They knew him here, and remembered his name. But when he started away from the order counter, his whole right leg went numb and he had to hold on to the counter to keep from spilling his drink. *Am I having a breakdown?* He managed to hobble to a nearby table where he pretended everything was normal, secretly rubbing the side of his leg, hoping for a return of feeling. Luckily they brought his order to the table so he didn't have to get up again until he left. The icy numb sensation had lessened enough to let him fake a "stroll" slowly back to his office.

Back at the office, he tried repeatedly to attack his workload. But his mind kept drifting. He must have opened the drawer where his phone was hidden nine or ten times, hoping for a message from Seth. Each time, the absence of any communication prompted another barrage of self-induced panic. He transitioned from worrying about what his wife and daughter would think of him to worring about what would happen to them if he actually went to prison.

He thought it likely that he could avoid prison or, at least, be given a very short sentence. He had enough in savings to buy a very good lawyer. Still a long legal battle would most likely exhaust a large part of that savings. Thankfully Cassie's little internet business would give them some support, but they'd have to move, and her business would likely suffer because of him. When they found out what some of the costumes had been used for, people might quit buying. *I have a good life insurance policy; maybe I can borrow against that to support my girls just for a year or so until I get out of prison.* As his mind nattered, he began to shake again, and the bottom of his foot felt almost numb with a weird hot/cold prickly feeling.

His mind wandered back to the prospect of prison. This one really scared him. He had heard that pedophiles and child pornographers got "special treatment" from the other inmates. He probably wouldn't have time to explain that he had never abused his daughter; he had simply shot some "artistic photos". Even though he was a very large man, he knew he couldn't keep himself safe in a prison. Maybe he would get sent to a Federal lockup where life was rumored to be less violent.

He sat paralyzed in his office waiting for everyone to go home. *I have to make a plan. I have to make a plan.* Natter, natter, natter.

As darkness fell, his plan began to pull together. There was only one honorable thing to do. He had to do it to save face for his little family. They didn't deserve to be ostracized because of him. He had tried to be a good father and husband. No, he wasn't perfect, but this thing was his only major failing through the years. All the little lies and occasional cheating, all the secret meetings with like-minded men, all those little things paled and melted away. He released them from the arsenal of darts that pierced his soul. Only this thing remained. He left a message with Cassie that he would be late, barely holding back a sob of grief. He changed into a polo shirt and cargo pants from the gym bag he kept in his office and went downstairs to his SUV.

Keith cried all the way across the bridge to Russellville. He had been raised out at Golden Pond and knew that side of Lake Dardanelle better than he knew the Dardanelle side. There was a little boat ramp just outside the Shiloh Park. The bottom had shifted to form a shallow bar just under the surface. He'd be able to walk out far enough that no one would see him.

There was a van with a boat trailor at the turn-around when Keith arrived, but no sign of anyone. To his surprise, a small boat with a trolling motor was tied to one of the trees on the bank. Keith guessed that the owner had gone in a car with friends for a quick bite in town. It took him about three seconds to decide to appropriate the boat. He untied it and stepped into it, pushing into the cold, cold water with one foot to launch himself. He couldn't get the trolling motor started, so he used the oar to gradually row farther out.

The water was a little choppy just before the evening calm, so it took him longer than he had esti-mated to reach what he knew to be deeper water. He sat alone, sobbing deeply now, contemplating his life, his family, and his predicament, slowly removing his shoes and socks. Finally he wiped the snot from his nose and stood up. He made one big jump over the side.

Something was wrong! He wasn't sinking fast enough. He had gained a good bit of weight this year, but he didn't think his beer gut would give him that much buoyancy. As he flailed in the water, he realized that the air pockets in his cargo pants were keeping him from completely submerging.

He struggled with the zipper and managed to kick them off along with his under shorts that were stuck to them. By then he was getting tired and was more than willing to sink into oblivion. How hard could it be to drown yourself?

It got harder fast. Just as he was going down with his lungs full of water, a spotlight hit him and several hands reached to tug him, naked ass and all, out of the water.

What Keith had missed in his haste to effect his demise was that the van was not empty. A middle aged couple had deferred loading the boat while they played a round of grab-ass in the back. As soon as they saw Keith start out with their boat, they called 911. The sheriff always had a boat and motor ready to go considering how many water accidents occurred in the area. The rescue team had roared down I-40 and launched off the little ramp by the time Keith got his pants off. Talk about bad luck!

The rescue team hurried Keith back to shore where EMTs worked on getting water out of his lungs until they were satisfied he was safe to transport. They ran with full lights and sirens to St.Mary's ER where he was checked out and put on a suicide watch in the psych ward. Far from being grateful, he was so humiliated he refused to give them his name (his wallet with ID was in the lake). They had to use the license on his SUV to identify him. The police department in Dardanelle, once contacted, tried again and again to contact his wife, but she was not answering her phone. Officers went to the house in case something such as a murder-suicide was in play, but found nothing.

45

Cassie was having a rough day. She had put her copy of Keith's computer stick in the laundry soap box for safe keeping. *Safe keeping for what?* She asked herself. Now she was really up against it. She could give the stick to the police and file for divorce. She could confront him with his crime and file for divorce. She could confront him and try to negotiate a better marriage contract. Or, she could simply file for divorce and threaten him with exposure if he failed to cooperate. The problem with just leaving him was that she would be leaving him free to continue his ugliness with someone else's child. Could she do that?

What will happen if he goes to jail or prison? What will happen to me and Candie? She forced herself to examine the scariest situation she'd ever been in. She had a lot to lose here. EVERYONE would know! She knew it wasn't her fault. Keith had done this all by himself; she was talking back to her fears the way Dr. Dintleman had taught her. Still, why did she feel that she had lost face? Because she lived in a culture where wifes were still blamed for their husband's failures. And, because her marriage was a failure. There were plenty of divorces on her side of the family, but she had believed that she would never get a divorce. She WOULD NOT be like them. She had chosen someone who was financially secure and had a good reputation in the community. How could this be happening? The answer was clear. SHE had made a poor choice.

MOVE!. Oh, God! She'd have to move. The house wasn't paid for. She could never afford it by herself. They had some money put away for emergencies, but it wouldn't begin to stretch more than a month or two. Besides, if he went to jail, there would be legal fees for him plus the cost of the divorce, eating up their resources, crumb by crumb. She remembered what had happened to her sister's finances with just the divorce part, no prison.

And Candie. *What will it do to Candie?* Someone would tell Candie that it was Cassie who had squealed, sending Keith to jail. Candie would never forgive her. Candie and her daddy were close (too close apparently). Dr Dintleman had described the relationship as one of co-dependence on Keith's part. He was hovering over Candie so he could keep control. God forbid that Cassie had control of their protégé. Dintleman had cautioned that if the relationship continued, as is, there was real danger of "fused egos". He described it as circles of self that rotated around everybody. When you interacted with someone, your circles overlapped a little. But with fused egos, the circles of self overlapped so much that it was hard to ever fully separate them.

Cassie sat drawing overlapping circles on the side of a tablet, shading in the zones of overlap. Suddenly she burst into tears that advanced to hysterical sobs as the magnitude of her broken heart flooded her emotions. She was still sobbing when her phone alarm went off. Time to go get Candie from pre-school. Time to pull herself together! She'd think about this later. Right now the pain was just too great.

Ice and makeup had repaired most of the damage to her face by the time Cassie pulled into the church parking lot for Candie. She kept her face turned away from the other parents as much as possible and was able to avoid any prolonged conversations. "Mommy," Cassie asked as they pulled onto the street, "what is this bag of peas doing in the car?"

"Oh," Cassie lied, "I bumped my head on the refrigerator door, and thought I'd try an old home remedy for the lump."

"Can I feel it?"

"It's right there," Cassie pointed to her hairline as the small fingers searched for a lump.

"I can't feel it."

"Good! The peas must have worked. Now where would you like to go to lunch today?"

"Umm," Candie was indecisive. She was much better at nixing her mother's choices than she was at picking something herself.

"I know," Cassie had a sudden idea, "let's go to Conway. We can get lunch at Busy Bees and maybe do a little shopping."

"Yeah, I guess," Candie agreed reluctantly. "But could we go to Chuckie Cheese instead of Busy Bees?"

"Yes!" Cassie smiled to herself. That was where she had planned to take the little manipulator to begin with.

The afternoon was actually fun when Cassie could get her mind off her situation. The pizza was mediocre, but the singing animals and the games were perfect for Candie. The little girl was fascinated by Whack-a-Mole. Cassie swatted at the fuzzy heads a few times for Candie's amusement, but she was afraid if she ever got started she might do some real damage. She remembered the roses she had annihilated yesterday.

They did a little shopping then had manicures and pedicures at Lady Love. While there, Cassie checked on the movie schedule, and they made the 4:00 matinee. Then they stopped at Walmart in Russellville to buy some yogurt and bananas for smoothies, and look at the baby clothes (one of the few safe areas for Cassie), and the toys, and the pet section (Candie wanted a puppy or a kitty), and the oral hygiene row, etc.

By the time they got home, it was well after dark so no wonder Cassie missed the police cruiser parked on her block. She had no sooner opened the door to hear the loudly ringing phone than a patrolman was on her door step.

46

When two patrolmen materialized on the steps, Cassie knew that she wasn't going to like whatever they told her. They asked if they could come in, and she offered them seats in the two overstuffed chairs while she sat on the sofa facing them. One of the officers was from Dardanelle, but the second, who took the lead in the conversation, was from Russellville. She sent Candie to the kitchen and out of ear shot to put away the one sack of groceries.

"Ma'am," asked the second patrolman, "is your husband Keith Kelly?"

Cassie nodded her yes.

"And does he drive a black Cadillac Escalade?" (He read the license number.)

"Yes." she finally spoke, "What's this about? Is Keith...," she trailed off.

"No, ma'am, he's all right now. But it was a very close call. About 7:30 this evening, he was pulled out of Lake Dardfanelle on the Russellville side. He had stolen a boat, and was apparently attempting suicide."

Cassie was silent. She put her head in her hands and stared at the floor. They had been at Walmart at 7:30, probably looking at baby clothes, while he was out in that cold water trying to make sure he'd never have another child. How weird was that?

She was totally dumbfounded. Yesterday she had wanted to kill him herself. Now this. "You say he's all right? Where is he now?" she managed to croak out the words.

"He's at St. Mary's in Russellville," the lead officer replied.

"Russellville? Why Russellville?"

"The ramp he went off is in Russellville. Actually, if he'd gone in over on this side, he might not have made it. The river is pretty fast on this side because of the dam."

"Can I see him?"

"No, ma'am," the officer replied. "He's under, er, he's being watched in case he tries it again. He'll be heavily sedated anyway, and might not even recognize you. Here's the number you can call first thing tomorrow morning." He handed her a card with the hospital number and the name of the doctor on call for the psychiatric ward (her own Dr. Norton). He also gave her his card with the number of the Russellville Police Department.

When the officers had gone, Cassie turned to see Candie peering around the corner with eyes so big she looked like a deer in headlights. "Mommie, what's wrong with Daddy?" the little girl sobbed as she ran to her mother.

You don't really want to tell her that, Cassie steeled herself. "Daddy's been in an accident, Honey. He's in the hospital in Russellville." *Keep it simple.*

Candie started wailing big time. "I want to see my daddy. He needs me! Why can't we go right now? I want to go now!"

"Shh, shh," Cassie held the little girl close, trying to sooth her. "Maybe you can see him tomorrow night, Baby."

Candie's response was to strike out, literally. Cassie caught the little fist just before it hit her face. "NO!" she pratically shouted at the little girl. "You do not hit me! Don't you ever try to hit me again. Go to your room. And don't you come out until you can apologize."

Candie's face was a complete vision of astonishment. With widened eyes and gaping mouth, she pulled away and made a bee line down the hall. The last thing Cassie heard was the slamming of the door.

Cassie was not happy with Keith. In fact she half wished he had been successful. Look what a mess he had created. There'd be some kind of newspaper article tomorrow or Thursday in both towns. She'd have to drag him around Russellville to get his SUV and a new driver's license. He'd have to deal with the rest of it himself. What to do? What to do? Well, at least she had an appointment with Dr. Norton Thursday.

47

Sophia had been sifting through all her leads that always lead to nowhere. On Tuesday she finally decided to tackle Dintleman's billing records herself, not knowing what she was looking for. Maybe something would pop up.

It did. When she looked back a year, not just at current patients, she discovered a Keith Kelly. He had been a patient for about two months. Then four months ago another Kelly, Cassie, had started seeing the doctor. Her research people had determined that Cassie was the owner of the Nissan Juke Bennie Sue had seen on that last Friday. Since Dr. Russell and Emily Leonard had seen Dr. Dintleman closer to his death than Cassie, Sophia had let that interview slide. Still, with the same address, Keith and Cassie were in all likelihood husband and wife. Why would they go separately? Why had Keith stopped? Why had Cassie started? Sophia remembered Dr. Russels's description of sometimes askew relationships when porn was involved. Could it be? She tried to contact Cassie to set up an appointment this week, but couldn't reach her. She'd try again tomorrow. Meanwhile she asked one of her team to find out what she could about Keith Kelly, including what kind of vehicle he owned.

48

Wednesday was a scary day for Keith. First he had to face the nurses who brought him breakfast in the morning. Then he had to talk to Dr. Norton, whom he despised by now, about his suicide attempt. Then he had to fill out paperwork without his wallet with his insurance and credit cards while he was still wearing a hospital gown, most of his clothes having sunk with him. Furtunately, one of the orderlies located an old, too small bath robe for him to stretch around himself.

He was allowed to use a phone on the ward, but Cassie either wasn't home or wasn't picking up. Here he was at the hospital totally humiliated, without proper clothes, or even shoes, being reduced to wearing slide-resistant socks on his feet. The hospital would release him and let him provide proof of insurance later. (A lot of good that would do. His insurance didn't provide mental health benefits.) At last out of desperation, he called his secretary at the bank in Dardanelle. She agreed to bring his dress shoes and socks that were still in his office and his dirty clothes (no underwear) from yesterday.

His secretary showed up about a half an hour later with his shoes and dirty clothes in tow. He quickly donned them and followed her down the elevator and through the labyrinth of halls out to visitor parking. He couldn't pick up his SUV because he didn't have any cash on him to pay the towing and impounding fees. Thankfully, he had a second set of keys at home since his main set was now at the bottom of the lake. He wondered, quite apart from anything relevant, how many sets of keys were down there now.

When he was dropped off at home in Dardanelle, he was grateful that Cassie wasn't there. He found the hidden house key and let himself in. There in the front hallway were all his clothes thrown into a pile. She was throwing him out! Oh, no, how could this be? Surely she didn't know about the photos of Candie. He rushed to his drawer. To his horror, it had been bashed in with the ballpene hammer that was still on the desk. The split fragments of kindling wood told the tale. His memory stick was gone! His Mont Blanc pen was out of place, and the felt lining was hanging over the edge of the empty box!

They know. They know They know. Got to get out of here! But how? Then it popped into his head. *You clever Devil*, he congratulated himself. He raced into the bedroom, shedding his clothes as he went. *Let her add these to the pile!* He was in anger mode now. He changed into running clothes and packed one change into the duffle bag he kept ready for beauty pageants. Then he hurried to the garage where he pulled out his ball glove and one of several bats. He rode his bicycle out into the street looking for all the world like some guy going to the park for a pick-up game. Instead of heading for the park, he pedaled to the edge of town and took Hwy-22W. He wasn't used to the cars whizzing by. They were especially worrisome since he imagined they were coming after him. He had to stop a couple of times to calm himself and catch his breath. He was careful to adjust his speed so he could turn down Bobcat Hollow when no cars were coming. He pedaled hard to get past the creek and turn into the lane where Dintleman's house was still marked off with police tape. Pushing his bike, he sauntered around to the back of the house where he leaned it against the side of the detached garage. He was almost home free. Using his all-purpose bat, he broke the glass in the back door and reached in to turn the deadbolt. Damn! The lock on the door was keyed!

He went back to the garage and began fiddling with the door lock there. He didn't have anything to pry the Quickset with so, in frustration, he gave the side door's handle a big whop with his bat. To his surprise, that did the trick. He quickly moved his bike inside and closed the door firmly.

There was very little light in the garage since the double-wide had no windows. But he could see enough from the two panes on the jimmied side door to find a few necessary things. He flipped on the light switch by the door just long enough to see that it was still working. Good if the electricity was on, chances were the water was too. Dintleman's antique Buick was in the garage, and the doors were unlocked. He could open a door and get enough dome light to search some more. There were the usual lawn tools and what appeared to be boxes of books. Keith was disappointed that Dintleman didn't have any camping gear. That was what he was really after.

There was a small refrigerator with a few bottles of water. Hastily gulping down a bottle, Keeith opened the freezer. It was stocked with microwavable meals, various hot dogs and sausages, some breads, and, of course, icecream. He'd have to come back to that later. He started to throw his empty water bottle into the trash can by the door, but decided to keep it in case he needed to make his own "golden bomb" during the night.

49

Wednesday, while Keith Kelly was trying to get out of the hospital, Sophia was on the trail. A dig into his particulars revealed his position at the bank, his partnership in Candie Kisses, and his ownership of a black Escalade.

Donny was passing by when he heard Keith's name through Sophia's office door. "Hey," he stuck his head into the office, "that's the guy who tried to commit suicide last night over at Russellville. Tried to drown himself. Rescue team got him just in time. They took him to St. Mary's, but he's probably gone by now. Rogers was on duty last night." Of course Rogers hadn't said anything to the day shift because he didn't know they had just started to look at Kelly.

Sophia digested the information for a minute then picked up her phone. Checking the number on her pad, she called Cassie Kelly again. This time Cassie was home and willing to talk to her. Sophia corralled Donny and quickly drove to the Kelly house.

A tearful Cassie with swollen eyes met them at the door and led them through the pile of Keith's clothing and assorted belongings into the living room. "I know it's a mess," she pointed out, waving her arm at the disheveled pile. "I'm throwing the bastard out!"

"And why would that be?" Sophia inquired in a tone that said this sort of thing happened all the time.

"He's...He's a sex offender." She collapsed into tears. "Let me show you." She turned and sadly walked into the laundry room, returning with a memory stick she was brushing free of powdered detergent. "Here, come with me." She walked across the hall to Keith's office. She inserted the stick and opened the picture files, selecting the one that had Candie and the rose in it.

"Oh, my," Sophia drew in her breath while Donny's eyes bugged out, "when did you find these?"

"Just this week."

"Are there others?"

"There have to be. I just don't know where. He keeps things in this drawer. I was just going to open it when you called." With that, she grabbed the ballpene hammer lying on the desk and bashed the front of the drawer into kindling. "Here, you have my permission to search this drawer," she said with a knowing finality.

Donny pulled on a pair of gloves and began pulling things out of the drawer. His experience with CSU led him to a much more thorough search than Cassie had made. It didn't take long for him to find the cache of SanDiscs under the felt lining of the

Mont Blanc box. There was a pile of green lockbox envelopes, probably for handling the discs.

"We're going to have to take these back to the station," Sophia explained. "Would you mind coming with us and making a statement?"

50

Keith spent a semi-miserable afternoon and night in the garage. He found a plastic spork from a fast-food restaurant in the glove compartment of the Buick. It wasn't much, but if he took his time he could gouge out bites of icecream without breaking the little points. He took out some bread and hotdogs and placed them in the little puddle of sunlight still coming through the door. Hopefully there was enough afternoon light still to come to thaw the hotdogs.

He was absolutely exhausted from his medications and the whole ordeal, so he climbed into the roomy back seat of the Buick, curled up into a fetal position, and conked out.

It was very late when he awakened. He pushed the phlorescent dial on the watch he had grabbed from the house: 2:00 am. Lots of time to make his plans. He opened the refrigerator just a crack and took our two bottles of water to slake his thirst. Propping the door so just a little light came out, he funbled his way over to the hotdogs. They were still cold, but not icy. He tore open the package of bread and gobbled several slices before wrapping a hot-dog in its makeshift bun. He closed the refrigerator and sat in the backseat again, wolfing down four hotdogs. Then he began to feel really queasy and lay down until the nausea passed.

The next time he awakened, it was almost 6:00 am. He carefully opened the door and sneaked to the back of the garage to relieve himself. He hoped there was an outside faucet he could use after the neighbors had gone to work. He really needed to wash himself. The odor of emotional sweat permeated his clothing and nearly gagged him.

He waited until 8:00 Thursday morning to be sure the neighbors were gone, then cracked the side door open. He gathered his duffle and sneaked to the back again. Hallelujah! There was a water spiggot, and the water had not been turned off. He took a hurried sponge bath in the icy cold water and shivered his way back into the garage. He had deoderant and a comb in his trip duffle, so he felt a little more human when he had finished.

His next big problem was the bicycle. He could ride the bike back into Dardanelle, no sweat, but what about making it to Russellville? He sensed that crossing the Arkansas River on a bike in four lanes of traffic could be dangerous. He needed wheels. Then it dawned on him. The Buick! It was an antique car, beautifully maintained and driven frequently. All he had to do was start it. He had become quite good at hotwiring cars when he was a kid. He had a pair of nail scissors and a file in his duffle. What else did he need?

He left the garage a little after 10:00, still chewing slices from his bread sack. He had put his bike in the back seat just in case. He threw his glove and bat and his duffle into the front and put his cap on backwards with the edge down nearly to his eyebrows. Hey, this was cool! Who needed suicide when he could be his own action figure? His spirits rose as he headed across the river. He was a man on a mission. He helped himself to another slice of bread.

He pulled in at the edge of the parking lot where Dr. Norton had his office in Russellville and waited. He knew Cassie usually saw the doctor around 11:00. He wanted to be early so he could confront her. When her Juke pulled into the lot at 10:50, he grabbed the bat and opened his door.

"Cassie!" he shouted, stopping her in her tracks.

She turned to see him advancing toward her with a baseball bat swinging at his side. Her terror was immediate. "You stay away from me!" she screamed. "The cops are looking for you, you pervert!"

A few people coming into and out of the building heard the yelling, and were curious enough to move in the couple's direction, but not curious enough to get involved.

As Keith got nearer, Cassie panicked and made a mad dash for the building. Keith cut her off and gradually backed her up against Dr. Norton's Mercedes. "This is what you deserve, you little bitch," he lifted the bat. Then he swung it full force into the front headlight of the car. "You're not going to take her away from me! You're not going to take her away from me!" he continued to scream as he bashed the car again and again.

Finally someone called 911 and he could hear sirens approaching in the distance. He slung the bat onto the grassy lawn and made a beeline for the Buick. He was blocks away before the police arrived.

Dr. Frank Norton came running out of his office when he heard his vehicle was being bashed to death. He found his next patient, Cassie Kelly, sitting on the curb beside his car bawling her eyes out. At first he thught she had done the damage, but quickly surmised that she lacked the strength. Then he spied the bat on the lawn. He started to pick it up, but hesitated. It might have fingerprints on it that would help catch the culprit.

When the Russellville police arrived and took statements from Cassie and several bystanders, one officer bagged the bat while the other put out a BOLO for Keith Kelley driving a very large red and brown Buick with 'antique car' license plates.

51

Bennie Sue didn't envision herself as a police officer. Her role in law enforcement was more technical. But she wanted police officers she trusted to be aware that the man she called "my pedophile" was alive and kicking. She had learned from her father and from the episodes with Beth Ann that something presented as seemingly innocent could be the pathway to child sexual abuse.

Bennie Sue had taken the SanDisc to Detective Cash who remembered her from 16 years earlier. He had been frustrated by his inability to use the evidence to nail Seth Gunter. He had seen many of the images on Beth Ann's camera years ago. The newer images convinced him that Seth was still on the job with the help of other pedophiles. The picture quality was very inconsistent and suggested multiple photographers.

Bennie Sue asked Detective Cash to forward a set of the images to Detective Sergeant Calypso at Dardanelle. Bennie Sue trusted Sophia and made an appointment to talk to her right after work

Wednesday. When Bennie Sue arrived it was evident that Sophia hadn't looked at her encrypted emails. She apologized and explained that police in the entire region were looking for Keith Kelly whose wife had finally dimed him out.

With Bennie Sue in the visitor's chair, Sophia opened her email. She had seen these pictures before. Today! They matched a set of pics from Kelly's library of SanDiscs. "And you're telling me that some of these pictures were taken by one of our faorite sex offenders, Seth Gunter?" She turned to her computer and began a file search of sex offenders by name. "Here, is this the man?" She asked, showing Bennie Sue earlier and current pictures of Seth Gunter.

Bennie Sue nodded, "I never knew his name. Those little girls at the beginning of the child pornography section took those pictures themselves because...what was his name? conned them into it 16 years ago. I'm the one who took the photos of the girls in the soap suds. And that little girl there," she motioned for Sophia to backup, "that's me. I feel so ashamed. It was bad enough then, but now who knows how many times perverts have looked at these during the past 16 years?" Her eyes began to tear.

"Well, there's some good news and some bad news in this mess," Sophia confided. "We found these pics just today on a memory stick from a suspect. The last picture on that stick was taken last week, according to the wife, and her husband made frequent trips to Conway, which is where we think Seth is holed up. Your pictures close the circle. The bad news is that we don't know the whereabouts of either Seth Gunter or our suspect."

Sophia held up a finger in the "wait a minute" signal and dialed her phone. She identified herself and began by asking, "Do you have any more news on Seth Gunter? I saw the BOLO this afternoon. No? Well, I'm sorry. We have reason to believe he has a buddy here in Dardanelle, and right now he's missing too. OK. Thanks, we'll keep you updated when we find something."

"Someone ratted Seth Gunter out yesterday. He's on the run, but who knows where. The best guess is he's out of the state by now. I hope he didn't come through here and pick up our guy. You just never know." Then she came back to Bennie Sue, "Girl, you are something else. After all you've been through you're still stepping up to the plate. If you ever need a letter of reference in the future, you can count on me!"

—⚁—

Seth Gunter was well on his way to Denver. He had some friends there who would believe he was just passing through and put him up for a few days while he made a new plan. As for Keith Kelly, he was sleeping in the back seat of Dintleman's antique Buick in Dintleman's garage behind Dintleman's house.

The Keith-monster had stayed well hidden until he appeared in Russellville Thursday morning waving a bat and screaming at his wife. The big red and brown Buick should have been an eye-catcher, but it disappeared as soon as it had appeared. He had to be hiding it somewhere close. Right now, the police had only his driver's license picture to go on, so they figured they'd better get the crime lab in Dardanelle to check for clues on the bat.

Bennie Sue signed the bat in and put it in her que with an ASAP request. (They were almost all ASAP.) She hoped to get to it today. Meanwhile the chatter around the lab was about some husband who was mad at Dr. Norton in Russellville and had pratically destroyed Norton's Mercedes with a baseball bat. The wife had collapsed, and the Paramedics had taken her to St. Mary's.

Meanwhile, Keith had returned to his garage hidey hole, but not before stopping at Mel's Bait Shop (no outside cameras) and picking up some supplies. He figured he'd better get out of there by noon tomorrow. With the weekend coming up, more people would be around in the nearby houses. For now he settled for a baloney sandwich with mustard, a chilled diet Pepsi, a small jar of jalapenos, and some corn chips.

When Bennie Sue finished lifting finger prints from the bat and photographing them, she gave the set to Steve Hoyle who was currently using the computer to search for matches among burglary suspects. The whole lab was startled when Steve began yelling, "It's him! It's him! He's our murderer!"

It took a while for police on both sides of the river to get it straight that the man who had tried to commit suicide Tuesday night, had been outed as a pedophile Wednesday, and had bludgeoned a Mercedes to death with a baseball bat on Thursday was one and the same person. Then the hunt began on both sides of the river in earnest.

It was the jalapenos that did Keith in in the end (so to speak). About 45 minutes after he'd eaten his evening allotment, they worked their magic. First, it was a feeling of bloating very much like bean gas. Then the pressure started to build in earnest, and finally outright IBS cramps took over. It was nearly dark when he sneaked out of the garage and ran to the back. He had just managed to get his pants down when the explosion came. The noise and ensuing odor was just enough to attract the doberman from next door, out for an evening run. When the dog stuck his cold nose up Keith's butt, Keith yelled and tried to jump away, but his trousers tripped him. As he struggled to get them up, the dog thought it was a game and began to pull and tug on the pockets.

By the time Keith kicked the dog away and pulled his pants up, the dog's owner was peeking around the back edge of the garage to see what his magnificent beast was wrestling with. The sight of the disheveled man and the smell of human feces alerted him that the situation was likely to be dangerous. He immediately ended his current call and dialed 911 while running back toward his own house and safety. His second call was to Dewey Elkins who was looking after the property until the estate was settled. "Dewey," he said, "you better get over here to Michael's. There's a strange man shittin' out behind the garage. Ain't no telling' what he's up to."

Dewey was at the house when he got the call. He immediately jumped into the Jeep and barreled across the intervening fields rather than take the road. His arrival was a good 10 minutes before the police. Dewey approached the back of the house carefully. He saw that the glass on the back door had been shattered, but saw no signs of entry. He turned toward the garage and saw that the lock had been damaged.

Not knowing if anyone was inside the garage, Dewey went back to his jeep and jammed it up against the big door with the lights on bright. Then he pulled a nine mm Glock out from under his sweatshirt, grabbed a flashlight from under the seat, and approached the side door. He slung the door open while executing a perfect dive and roll in case the intruder had a gun. He searched all around the garage. Clearly someone had been squatting here. But he didn't see anyone. He turned cautiously to hunt outside. Maybe the intruder had run into the bushes behind the huse. Then he heard something.

When Keith saw the lights from outside, he panicked and crawled back into the Buick's back seat, pulling an old lap robe over his shaking body. He heard little noises that told him someone was looking around the walls. He prayed no one would think to look inside. It got really quiet. Then the footsteps headed toward the side door. The pressure was building up in his guts again. If he could just hold it until the side door closed. Then pfffttt! Pfffttt even louder. He couldn't stop it.

At first Dewey couldn't believe his ears. *It can't be. Can it?* He approached the car stealthily and flung the back door open. His gun was pointed directly at a shaking, farting blob. "Come out of there, you," he commanded. And Keith Kelly was toast.

52

It took several weeks to get everything straightened out. There was plenty of evidence to convict Keith of possession, production, and distribution of child pornography, with or without Seth Gunter who was now in the wind. As for murder, there were the fingerprints on the two bats, and the shoe size fit the print in the wine at the scene. But they were still trying to figure out the motive. Keith wasn't talking to anyone. Based on his week's activities, he was on suicide watch at the jail. He was still ranting about somebody taking "her", but the dots weren't connecting.

Interviews with Cassie were helpful, but not definitive. She had talked to both Dintleman and Norton about her plans to leave Keith because of the porn, but she hadn't known about the child porn until just before his suicide attempt. Perhaps Keith thought she had said something about child pornography to one or both counselors. Then the "her" would be Candie. He would lose her if Cassie left.

The disposition of Dintleman's estate would be pretty much *pro forma*, although it would take time to work through the probate court. As a verifiable daughter, Bennie Sue would inherit the house which had been paid for by Bennie Sue's grandmother. She would also inherit the approximately $200 thousand TIAA retirement account because the beneficiary was listed as "my trust". Dewey would receive the $100 thousand life insurance policy that listed him as the beneficiary. And Dewey had agreed to be the estate's executor.

Bennie Sue was overwhelmed by the reality of her change in fortune. What in the world would she do with her new wealth? It was as if she had won the lottery. Relatives and friends and needy cases started popping up all around her. She decided to sell the house. Her first impulse had been to give it to Della who deserved better than she had received. Then Bennie Sue tried to imagine Della in the house and changed her mind. She envisioned the house going to seed because Della didn't have the resources to keep it up. There would be loud drinking parties and any number of men parading in and out of her mother's life, not to mention Cheyenne and her circle of friends.

Not going to happen! After some tortured thinking about family and duty, Bennie Sue made up her mind. She would offer to pay for Della's rehab and provide her with her usual income while she was in. Cheyenne would get full tuition for any university she wanted to attend. She was on her own for room and board. Work was probably the only thing that would keep her honest. Aunt Alexis would get a one-time gift of $50 thousand. That would give her enough to take some of those trips she had always dreamed about, or maybe art workshops were more her style now.

And Bennie Sue? She wasn't sure. She had several ideas she wanted to talk over with her friends.

At the next Friday lunch, the other women asked Bennie Sue outright what she planned to do with her money. "Hang onto it until you have a solid plan," Hattie advised.

"Yeah, I know," Bennie Sue returned. "I've been studying the pitfalls of lottery winners. It's amazing the messes people get themselves into once they win a few million dollars! I've been thinking about booking one of those rocket flights to the moon."

"You'll need more than that," Rachel said laughingly. "Come on, what are you really thinking about?"

"Well," Bennie Sue gulped, "I think I'll go back to school. I want to help with the child abuse problem. I really do. It seems as if abuse and pornography have been tracking me most of my life. But I'm not sure where I want to put my energy. I'll make a decision this summer then start applying to graduate schools this fall for next year."

"How much longer does Jeff have?" Garnet was very perceptive.

"Um," Bennie Sue wavered, "just one year. Then he's willing to go wherever I go."

"You rascal, you've been holding out on us!" Hattie exclaimed. "Is this your way of giving me a year's notice?"

"Who's been holding out?" Just then Sophia Calypso joined the group. She had come directly from the beauty shop where she had changed her hair back to its original color and had it cut into a short, very flattering easy care style.

"It looks as if you've been holding out!" Rachel looked at her from across the table. "Since when have you been a red head?"

"I've always been a red head. This is my natural color. I changed it when I started at the Academy. When I was tending bar, guys were always teasing me about it and coming on to me. I wanted them to take me more seriously."

"Well, who's coming on to you now?" Bennie Sue asked with a twinkle in her eye. "Could it be a certain half-uncle I know?"

Sophia didn't respond. She didn't have to. They all knew the answer.

The End

AN EXCERPT FROM

BERYL WEALAND'S

UPCOMING BOOK

IDENTITY OF DEATH

IDENTITY OF DEATH

Dr. Garnet Daniels was having a particularly pleasant day. She loved teaching Human Gross Anatomy for the med students. Today was the first lab, the day the students met their cadavers for the first time. Fifty students had started this morning. Now it was time for the second batch of 50 to begin the time honored process.

Students assembled around each table in groups of four, cracking crude jokes and trying to not show their discomfort with actually touching their first cadaver. The dissecting groups would coat their cadaver's face with Vaseline and wrap the head in gauze. This procedure would help keep the facial tissues moist until later in the semester when students had acquired enough skill and finesse to complete the tedious dissection of the face.

But first, the names were read. There was always the possibility that a student might have known a particular cadaver. That cadaver would be removed and exchanged with one that was not known in order to avoid a potentially traumatic experience. The names having been read, all identifiers were removed from the table, and the students began the Vaseline and gauze process.

Garnet was giving group five a little assistance when she heard a sharp intake of breath from Dr. Bradshaw, one of her fellow teachers. When she looked up, Morry Bradshaw was quite pale, and his eyes were glued to the female on the table. He was definitely alarmed! Garnet rushed over to assist Morry. When she saw the cadaver, she looked at Morry, then at the cadaver, then at Morry. As their eyes locked, Garnet's quick thinking helped mobilize Dr. Bradshaw.

"Oh my," she blurted, "we're not supposed to use her. She was selected for the surgeons in-service because she exhibited lymph edema when she died."

"You're right. I knew there was some mix-up," Morry Bradshaw ad-libbed. "Hang on," he addressed the four-student dissecting team. "We'll get you a different cadaver. Damn surgeons are so picky."

Mr. Hartman, the department's embalmer/denier knew that the surgeons were not coming until next week and that they would require a fresh, unembalmed cadaver to practice various surgical approaches. Nevertheless, he sensed Dr. Bradshaw's mild panic and played along. Cadaver five was removed and replaced with another female. The goal was to provide about equal numbers of males and females for the students.

The remainder of the lab progressed as usual. Once the faces were wrapped, the next chore was to place each cadaver in the prone position (face down). The muscles of the back were relatively large, and would survive the misdirected hacking of the novice dissectors. Although the students had been given gloving and safety instructions, Garnet held her breath as she witnessed one aggressive young man use a scalpel to slice away some superficial fascia. He froze as the tips of his gloves fell off, revealing the ends of his fingers mere millimeters away. He took a deep breath, put the scalpel down, and carefully proceeded with dissecting scissors. Lesson learned!

As soon as the last student pushed through the door with his shoulders, holding both hands up and sniffing the unmistakeable odor of cadaver, Morry and Garnet made a beeline to the rejected cadaver which Mr. Hartman was uncovering for them.

"It can't be!" Morry burst out.

"But it is. I'd know her anywhere. That's Beth Justice. She worked here five years. And the irony is that she directed the Donated Body Program. How in the world did this happen? What name did she come in under?"

Mr. Hartman held up the donated body papers, "Edna Summermann, with two m's and two n's," he read the name.

About The Author

Beryl Wealand is the pen name of Paula B. Pendergrass, Ph.D. Dr. Pendergrass is retired from the Biology Department at Arkansas Tech University and currently lives between Russellville and Dover, Arkansas. Her alter ego, Dr. Garnet Daniels, is aided by relatives and friends in solving mysteries surrounding Arkansas River Valley events. The professionals and local characters in Beryl's books are drawn from memories created during many years of teaching and living in the Ozark Mountains.